A BED OF BLADES

Other books by Kate Avery Ellison include:

A Gift of Poison (The Kingmakers' War #1)

Frost (The Frost Chronicles #1)

Thorns (The Frost Chronicles #2)

Weavers (The Frost Chronicles #3)

Bluewing (The Frost Chronicles #4)

Aeralis (The Frost Chronicles #5)

The Curse Girl

Of Sea and Stone (Secrets of Itlantis #1)

By Sun and Saltwater (Secrets of Itlantis #2)

With Tide and Tempest (Secrets of Itlantis #3)

For Wreck and Remnant (Secrets of Itlantis #4)

In Dawn and Darkness (Secrets of Itlantis #5)

Once Upon A Beanstalk

A BED OF BLADES

KATE AVERY ELLISON

ISBN-13: 978-1523907038

ISBN-10: 1523907037

For Scott

ONE

THE HUNTRESS WAS losing.

The tavern was packed with as many people as it could hold. Trappers, merchants, and villagers alike crowded around the table, drinking ale and giving advice as the players studied their cards—the huntress, her sharp eyes growing more slitted with every play, a trapper with thick black hair and a too-smooth face that clashed with his rough fur coat, and a thin, dirty guttersnipe girl. The watchers favored the trapper and the huntress equally in their bets, and the ones who'd placed money on the huntress muttered and cursed at her recent luck.

Briand had always been good at knowing when others were approaching the end of their patience, particularly with her. In this case, she knew she had perhaps one more game of Dubbok in this tavern before someone decided to pull a knife.

The trapper had initiated the game, boasting that he was the finest card player in the wild province. The huntress had challenged that claim after a few swigs of ale. The whole tavern had laughed when Briand announced herself the best Dubbok player in Kyreia, the Northern Province, and so she'd promised to prove it.

Now, they jeered her.

The huntress stared at her cards with a scowl on her face, and Briand kept her features composed as she waited for the woman's move. The pile of coins in front of the huntress had dwindled to nearly nothing.

Beside the huntress, the trapper scratched his smooth chin with the back of his knife. His pile of coins was the largest.

The huntress placed a card down in front of her. A king, a good card, but poorly employed since she had no other members of the royal suit.

"Lords," she muttered, "I'm not used to this backwater method of playing Dubbok, with no dealer and no caller and no proper table."

The trapper snorted as he perused his hand. "This here is the truest version, the way the game was meant to be played. If you want to play with gloves on, go sip tea in Cahan's capital."

Everyone present muttered at the mention of Cahan, and a few spat on the ground.

"Not inside!" the tavern keeper groused at them.

The trapper slapped down the priest card, earning a murmur of appreciation from the audience peering over his shoulders.

"There," he said with satisfaction. "I believe that gives me the winning number."

All eyes turned to Briand.

The trapper grinned, showing his teeth.

Briand's expression didn't change. She ran her finger over the edge of the well-worn card in her hand, letting the moment stretch along with the trapper's smile. This was the delicious pause where the opponent believed he'd won. She breathed it in as she fixed her eyes on him. *Witch's eyes*, her uncle had claimed once. The effect seemed to be the same on the trapper, and his smile faltered for a second.

She laid down her card.

The waif.

The huntress pressed her fingertips to her mouth.

"Normally a useless card," Briand said to the trapper, speaking for the benefit of any watcher who didn't know the rules. She'd hate for anyone to miss the import of the play. "Of course, in the northern version—by your own admission the true version— the waif, if there's no courtesan in play, becomes an orphan and takes all the power from the priest. It's an obscure play, but of course, you know it, being the finest player in the province, after all."

A few people tittered.

Briand reached for the pile of money with one hand.

The trapper grabbed her wrist. "You cheating little guttersnipe," he hissed.

Briand slammed her knife into the table, barely missing his arm. The handle quivered. The trapper loosened his grip, startled, and she yanked out of reach.

The air thickened as they stared at each other. Briand lifted an eyebrow, exuding calm, although her heart pounded in her ears. "Cheating?"

The knife was still quivering in the middle of the table.

He straightened, brushing his hands down his coat. "That card," he snapped, "wasn't in my deck."

"You're right," Briand said. "I saw that you'd removed it, and I put it back in."

The crowd giggled nervously. The trapper sat back as she collected the coins, and the huntress tipped her head toward Briand in acknowledgment. She was smiling, seemingly cheered by the trapper's loss. "Well played. I salute you, guttersnipe," she said.

Briand kicked back her chair and stood. She plucked her knife from the table and turned to go. Turning her back was a risk, but also a sign of confidence. The back of her neck tingled, and she put her hand on the knife at her waist in anticipation, but shame and the weight of so many eyes must have kept the trapper in his seat. The crowd parted, and Briand stepped from the tavern into the icy air of the street. The coins jingled as she walked.

She headed for the docks, where the sound of hammers rose from the mist along the water. Gillspin curved like a sickle around a natural harbor. Wooden houses with roofs topped with moss formed a maze of walkways and paths down the mountainside to the water's edge. Wash fluttered half-frozen across the roads, the ends stiff with frost. Gulls screamed overhead. The wind off the mountain was fresh, but it caught the scent of rot as it blew through the temporary settlement of tents that formed the fever colony where those afflicted with spotted fever were banished to recover or die. Lately, that scent of rot had hung over the whole city.

This place had been Briand's home for nearly a year now. She did not intend to make it two.

The scent of snow hung on the wind even though it was early summer, and suddenly memories filled her head. She drew in a ragged breath, and for a moment, it was as if she was back on the horse reaching with her mind to meet the dragon's. An ancient and consuming hunger swept through her before memory faded, and she was once again on the street in Gillspin, clutching the wall, trembling.

Before she could recover from the flash of memory, a hand seized her wrist and yanked her into a side alley. Briand kicked and fought, but she was overpowered by two figures in cloaks and hoods. She recognized them from the crowd at the tavern as the one holding her tipped her chin up to meet his face. Her skull scraped stone.

"Give us the money," the one holding her said, pressing his hand against her throat until she coughed and gagged.

She spat in his face, and he backhanded her across the cheek. The other reached out and yanked the coin purse from her belt. They shoved her to the ground and ran for the mist, and she let them go without pursuit.

When they'd vanished, Briand climbed to her feet and felt her neck for injuries.

She hated Gillspin. It was nothing but a garbage pit for rats and thieves. She couldn't leave soon enough.

She headed for home, her throat throbbing as she wove between pilings and underneath walkways. When she neared the water, an old man sitting on a stack of barrels stuck out his walking stick and poked her shoulder.

"Alms," he demanded, and coughed. "I fear I might have spotted fever. Help me."

"Hello, Fish," Briand said wearily.

The old man dropped the act. "You look wretched. What happened? Someone jumped you, didn't they?"

She didn't reply.

He spat at the ground. Everyone in Gillspin was overly fond of spitting. Another reason to hate the place. "They jumped you." It was a declaration now. "I've told you a hundred times not to take the back way to the docks when you're carrying coin."

"I like the back way," she said. "I can see the whole lake from it."

He grumbled under his breath, and she only caught bits of his insults—foolhardy gutter girl, ninny maid, tenacious rat, wasteful sprite.

"Hold your insults," Briand said, offended. She parted the front of her garment to reveal the second bag she wore around her neck. "I didn't waste a single coin. The one they got was full of river stones. I'm not stupid."

Fish cackled as she tossed him his cut, a single copper, and slipped the rest back into her shirt. "You're a sly one, Guttersnipe," he said, moving his feet from the lowest barrel to allow her passage.

Briand placed one boot on the barrel and kicked it back to reveal a tunnel beyond. Her feet found the well-worn steps leading down, and she descended into the darkness below.

She almost stumbled over an unconscious body on the steps. It stirred, squinting, and a beam of light caught a dirty face with a torn ear and a missing tooth.

"Rook," she said. "You've mistaken the ground for your bed again."

Rook groaned and grudgingly made way. "But it's so soft." He patted at the stones absentmindedly while he flashed her the same grin that netted him coppers from sympathetic travelers when he begged at the docks.

The grin didn't work on Briand. She was impervious to sleazy louts thanks to her uncle, not that he'd ever tried to bestow any charm on her.

"That's due to all the fleas you have bedding down with you."

Rook sighed. "So callused." He caught Briand's sleeve. "Any spare coin?" The grin made a second appearance, lingering this time.

"No," she said. "You'll only gamble it away."

"You gamble," he protested. "You play Dubbok every day with the traders."

"Yes," Briand said, "and I win."

He didn't deny the truth of her insinuation, but he looked like he was trying to think of a way to do so convincingly.

"Besides," she added. "I'm saving up." She continued on, and Rook trailed her, stumbling a little on the steps.

"Don't lie to yourself, Guttersnipe," he called. "You aren't going to get out of here. Nobody leaves once they fall in with Rag. Whatever your life was before, it's over now. You're one of us. Might as well sweeten everyone's pot and make some friends."

Instead of replying, Briand grabbed a low-hanging beam and swung over the sewer line. A row of stone arches beyond opened to a room shaped like a well, round and lined with stones, with a cascade of light pouring down from a hole in the ceiling.

She had to pay her tax to the thief-queen.

In the center of the round room, a woman with silver hair and eyes as cutting as broken glass sat on a throne built from barrels and pallets. She wore three layers of clothing, bits of each subsequent layer peeking through the holes and tatters of the others. Her boots were caked in mud, and she wore fingerless gloves over her long, scarred hands. Shadows pooled in the hollows and angles of her eyes and nose, making her face look like a skull. The light glinted in her bedraggled hair.

Rag, the thief-queen of Gillspin.

A line of unfortunates waited for an audience with her, and so Briand rested her shoulders against the wall to wait her turn. She scanned the others—a stone-faced old man with a girl beside him. A pickpocket dressed in plain browns and carrying a dozen pouches. A figure in a gray cloak, the hood drawn up over the head and the face in shadow.

Briand knew the hooded figure. She shifted her weight, feeling the comforting press of her knife at her hip.

Rag beckoned to the old man and the girl, and the old man shoved the child forward.

"I cannot feed her anymore," he said as the child sniffled. "I have my own debts to tend to."

"We are not a charity house—" Rag began.

"She's quick with her fingers and she's a fast learner. She could lift coins from the merchants, or scrub floors, or beg."

"Don't tell me how to make use of my thieves," Rag said coldly. She looked at the girl, her head cocking to the side.

The girl sniffled again, but she quieted under the sudden scrutiny. Tears dripped from her cheeks to the front of her shirt. She was barefoot, her legs and toes caked in mud. She couldn't have been older than eight.

"Her mother's dead," the old man added. He rubbed his left ear as he spoke, a nervous tic perhaps. "She knows her letters and numbers and how to write her name. She's clever as a robin, this one is. I'll part with her for three silvers."

"Is this man your father?" Rag asked the girl.

"She doesn't—" the old man began.

Rag silenced him with a gesture. She looked at the child, who shook her head with a swish of dark hair. She said something softly.

"What's that, child?" Rag said.

The girl repeated herself, her lips shaping the word.

Uncle.

Briand felt cold. She leaned forward, looking closer, and her eyes narrowed as she saw the bruises on the girl's arms.

Rag's eyebrows lifted lazily. She focused on the old man again, asking him another question, but Briand couldn't hear over the pounding of her heart in her ears.

15

"Three silvers, you say?"

Everyone turned and looked, and she realized she hadn't just thought the words, but shouted them. She stood in the light, bathed in their stark stares. Even the hooded man was watching her.

The old man smiled eagerly at Briand's query. He nodded, his head bobbing. "You won't be sorry. I've only had her a year in my care, but she's always eager to please. She'll be a goldmine for you, might make a good bride to a merchant when she's too old to beg..."

Briand's mouth curled. She felt sharp and hard all over, every bit of skin like the point of a knife, ready to draw blood.

He kept talking, rubbing his ear, smiling nervously, greedily, out of the side of his face. "If she serves you half as well as me, you'll double that money in a few months' time. If you don't, she responds well to the whip. Just like a dog."

Something in Briand snapped. "I'll pay it," she said.

TWO

THE ROOM WENT silent as Briand's words rang out like stones flung into an empty well.

The little girl sniffed loudly. The old man smiled and scratched his neck. The thief-queen focused on Briand, a glint of interest firing behind her eyes. "Why the sudden interest, Guttersnipe?"

Uncle. The word was like a whispered curse. Briand shook her head with a jerk. She wasn't discussing her motives.

Rag didn't seem to care to press the matter. After a glance at the old man, she flicked a finger, and two thieves came forward to flank the man and child.

"For four pieces—" the man began.

One of the thieves drew his knife with a hiss of metal against leather.

"None of that," Rag said. "If one of my own wants her, then so be it. You want a bidding war, you go to the docks. Not here."

He muttered something and spat on the ground.

Briand reached into her pouch and withdrew three coins. She threw the money down.

The old man snapped his fingers, and the girl dropped to her knees to pick it up. She offered it to him, and he reached for it.

Rag yawned, watching as the man plucked the money from the child's palm. "Now get out," the thief-queen said pleasantly. "Don't come back. We won't return her."

The old man scuttled away, and Briand realized suddenly that she'd just bought herself a child, and she hadn't the slightest idea what she was going to do now. She glanced around at the others as a sinking feeling clutched her stomach.

"A little servant girl for you, Guttersnipe?" Rag asked.

The girl had stopped crying and was gazing at Briand. Her eyes were large and solemn in the middle of her pale face.

"Make her a thief," Briand said, the words coming out clipped. "I don't... I don't want her for anything."

Rag shrugged and smiled at the girl, and it was a frightening sight, all pointed teeth. The girl didn't smile back.

"You will be safe here," the thief-queen said. "Pick a name, and pick well, as it will be yours for the rest of your stay here. Something simple, something descriptive. We're all thieves and beggars. We don't have fancy titles."

"Lark," the girl whispered. She darted a look at Briand, as if for approval.

"Welcome, Lark," Rag said, a simple bestowment, a ceremony and invitation and christening all in one. She motioned to one of the thieves, a tall and hulking man with scars across his arms. "You had a daughter, didn't you? Show the girl around. Make sure she learns the ropes."

The thief guided the girl away, and Briand returned to the wall, pulse singing in her ears, skin hot. She let her head fall back against the stones and drew in a breath.

18

The next in line, the pickpocket, parceled out a few of his pickings and poured them in a bucket at Rag's feet. After he retreated into the shadows, the figure in the gray cloak stepped forward, a whisper of cloth in the dim light. Rag lifted her chin.

"You are not one of mine," she said. "Have you come to sell me a child-bride too?"

"I seek only a night's lodging," the figure said in a husky, low voice. A man.

Rag tipped her head. "There are inns in Gillspin, stranger. Why come to me?"

"There is protection among your thieves, I hear."

She snorted. "They'll lose an eye if they rape anyone, and they're thrown out for murder, but otherwise, they are a loose rabble."

The man shrugged with one graceful motion of his shoulder. "Perhaps I want the company of a rabble. I seek to stay in the shadows."

Rag smile was just a slow curl of her lips. She nodded at the bucket, and the cloaked man dropped a stream of copper into it. He didn't count the coins as they fell, but the gift was generous. He gave a slow tip of his hooded head before he drew back, and Briand heard Rag say, "Enjoy a seat at my table for a night, stranger."

Then he was gone, and she focused on Briand, who pushed off the wall and came to stand in the center of the room where the light illuminated her.

Rag's eyes glimmered as she leaned forward.

"Ah, Guttersnipe," she said. "What do you bring me in exchange for the safety of my patronage?"

"I just gave you a new thief," Briand said.

"Well, that was a gift. It does not negate your toll," Rag said.

Briand drew out the pouch and poured half the coppers into her palm, and then dropped the coins into the bucket at the foot of Rag's throne. They rattled against the other coppers.

Rag smiled, showing her pointed teeth. "Enjoy at seat at my table for another night."

The customary words.

Briand backed away until the shadows ate her up and she was enveloped, and then she made her way to the great chamber with arching aqueducts that formed an X in the center of the room. Once an ornate bathhouse, now a ruin. Fingers of dying sunlight striped the floor through the slats in the wooden ceiling, which formed part of the boardwalk street above. Tables ran the length of the room, piled with baskets of bread and fish, and the voices of thieves rang out with humor and indignation as bedraggled young men and women ate and argued.

Briand found an opening at one of the tables and snagged a cup of mulled cider and a plate of sweet rolls, stuffing them with bits of fish and honey before retreating to beneath one of the aqueduct arches to eat. She leaned back, resting her head against the stone arch. The cider warmed the back of her throat and loosened her joints, unspooling the tightness that bound her stomach. Normally she didn't indulge in the cider, not if she wanted to keep her wits sharp, but the business with the old man and the girl had dredged up something sharp and painful in her.

The little girl from before perched on a bench at the end of one of the tables, a plate of bread before her. Briand watched the girl as Lark took a bite of one of the sweet rolls, her mouth like a doll's, pale and pink. A few of the other thieves watched the girl speculatively, but the one Rag had assigned to watch Lark glowered at them. He was tall and thick, and his pockmarked face looked as though it had been hewn from rock with an axe. Briand remembered his name: Crag. His story, like all the thieves', was a mystery, because histories were points of leverage. No one in the thief-queen's underground talked about their past, or even their name, but it was rumored that his daughter had been killed by huntsmen of the usurper prince.

They sat there, the little girl with a face like an angel and the hulking man with the body of a beast, and a pocket of solitude surrounded them. Something twitched in Briand's chest, a twinge akin to loneliness. She bit into her sweet roll and swallowed hard, the bread scraping her throat and making her eyes water.

When she'd finished eating, her head was too fuzzy and sleep promised oblivion from the sadness. She headed for the tunnels.

The little girl jumped up to follow her, her face a mixture of worshipful devotion and fear.

Briand turned swiftly. "What are you doing?" Her voice came out harsher than she'd intended. Conversations trailed off. Individuals turned, set down their cups. Everyone was watching, leaning forward. The burn of their stares pressed against her.

Lark faltered, blinking. "I... You bought me. I should go with you."

Rook appeared at Briand's elbow, his face too close to her shoulder as he leaned in. "Yes, you had coin to spend on this little wretch. Why not me? I told you I needed it. I—"

"I don't have any coppers for you," she snapped at Rook.

The girl, Lark, was still gazing at Briand.

"You're free," Briand said to her, disgust at the mess she'd created tightening around her neck like a noose. Should've left well enough alone.

"I don't want to be free. I want to belong to someone."

"Then stay with Crag. Just leave me alone."

The words seemed to smack the child like stones. She recoiled from them, her lip trembling.

"Should've given the money to me," Rook said.

Briand was gripped with loathing, for herself and Rook and the entire room of thieves with their bright eyes and curious, hungry smiles.

"Shut up, Rook," she said, pulling out her knife. But her hand trembled. She didn't want to fight. She whirled and plunged into the shadows of the corridor beyond.

The darkness wrapped her up and made her feel safe. The voices faded into the echoing silence. The dusty air swirled around her. She sheathed her knife and leaned against the wall to breathe.

The shadows stirred and took shape. She tensed, hand back on the knife, poised to run.

It was the hooded man from before, the man who had purchased shelter for the night with words of persuasion and a fist full of coin. He reached out a hand, and she spotted the tattoo of a lion on his wrist, the tail curling down to his fingers.

She knew him, but not his face. She made no move to run. He'd come here to speak to her, that much she knew. In the time since her abandonment, she'd had to make deals. Arrangements. Anything to save her skin, because she was on her own now.

The Hooded Man was part of one such arrangement. She loathed him for it.

"You could have kept the girl, made her your accomplice," the Hooded Man said. His voice was a curl of smoke in the quiet, husky and languid, but it had an edge to it.

Briand ran one finger down the handle of the knife at her belt. "I don't take accomplices. I work alone."

"Why?"

She could make out the tip of a nose, the hint of a chin. She'd never seen his face.

"Because you can't trust people," she snarled. "They always leave in the end, and what are you left with? Brokenness, worse than ever before. It's a fool's game to form alliances like that."

She thought of Kael, Tibus, and Nath. Her cousin, Bran. Her chest tightened, and nausea rose in her throat. She'd loved them, and for what? They'd left her with the Hermit, and she'd stayed, waiting for them to return as they'd sworn they would.

They hadn't.

They'd abandoned her. She'd never thought she could trust anyone. Perhaps that was why it hurt so deeply.

She realized the cider had loosened her tongue, and she felt foolish. "Why are you here?" she snapped.

"I was in the area on... business," he said softly. "I thought I would see if you'd kept your end of our bargain."

"I haven't had the chance," she said.

"You might find the opportunity sooner than you think."

She only laughed at that idea, a harsh sound in the darkness. He was wrong.

She had nothing more to say to him, so she crept away to where her bedroll was stashed atop of ledge of stone in one of the furthest chambers of the underground. Once curled on the bedroll, alone and out of the sight of any of the other thieves, Briand counted the coppers twice to make sure she hadn't made any mistakes, then poured the coppers back into the bag and put the bag under a loose stone in the floor.

She had been working on her stash for a long time. She had acquired nearly the amount she needed to pay for passage back to Kyreia, even with her generous purchase of the girl.

She covered the stone with a patch of hay and put her pillow over it, then lay down and gazed up at the ceiling of earth and dirt. A crack scarred the view, a tiny fissure that let in a streak of light from the street above and droplets of water when it rained. For a while, snakes and lizards had always seemed to find their way inside to her, but she'd eventually learned how to keep from attracting them all the time like a wildflower bringing bees.

Briand scooted onto her side and shut her eyes. Hope crawled through her, a pitiful but persistent prisoner in her head.

Soon she would catch a ship and be gone from this place.

~

Briand awoke to a dark shape above her and fingers over her mouth. She bit down hard on the hand, tasting blood as her assailant screamed. She kicked him off and scrambled up to fight.

Someone else grabbed her from behind, twisting her arm, pulling her off the bedroll in the darkness. She struggled, but this time she couldn't break the hold.

The attacker shoved her against the wall and groped for the money pouch around her neck as Briand felt for her knife. He found her blade and laughed as he waved it in front of her face.

"Looking for this?"

"Don't hurt her. We just want the money," someone else called.

Rook's voice.

The one holding Briand pressed the knife to her throat. His voice was deep and raspy. "Where's the money, Guttersnipe?"

Briand didn't answer.

He pushed the blade deeper into her neck, breaking the skin. Blood trickled down her collarbone.

A shout came from behind them, and then the Hooded Man was in their midst. He yanked the assailant away from Briand and struck him across the face. The others were already disappearing into the dark.

Briand caught herself against the wall and grabbed her knife from the ground as the one who'd attacked her fled. Her bedroll lay huddled in a heap, the straw strewn about. Briand dropped to her knees to check for her coins. Had they taken them? Desperation strangled her until she found them, still hidden, and she could breathe again.

The Hooded Man straightened his cloak. His movements hadn't even disrupted the hood that concealed his face.

"Are you unscathed?" he asked.

"Why'd you help me?" Briand was still on her knees, the coins clenched in her hands. The Hooded Man wasn't a person of kindness. She didn't trust him. She had good reason not to.

"You haven't completed our part of the agreement," he said.

Briand noticed Lark standing in the passage.

"What are you looking at?" Briand snapped at her.

"I told that man to help you because you were being robbed." Lark pointed at the Hooded Man. "I saved you."

She said it proudly, earnestly, as if such a gesture of loyalty was bound to be honored with eternal friendship.

Sudden tears prickled Briand's eyes. That wasn't how this wretched world worked. Friends didn't stay. They used and abandoned. The sooner the girl learned that, the better off she'd be.

"Then consider any debt you feel toward me repaid." Briand grabbed her coins and shoved her way toward the halls to report Rook's deeds to the thief-queen.

THREE

DAWN LOOKED LIKE dried blood against the blackish sky as the cold wind from the lake whipped tendrils of Briand's hair into her eyes and made them sting. Around her, the city was beginning to stir as smoke curled from chimneys and dogs rooted through trash in the alleyways. A clatter of horse's hooves sounded on the cobblestones of the road beyond.

She reached the edge of the lake and climbed down between the docks to get at the smooth, flat stones that lay scattered along the shoreline. She worked quickly, selecting the flattest, smoothest ones that could pass for coins if her bag was snatched in an alley again. She ground her teeth together as she worked. She felt swollen and heavy, blistered with fury and weighed down by dread. The attack last night had rattled her.

She couldn't wait to be gone from this place.

Rook had fled. She'd visited the miserable hole that he used as a sleeping place as soon as the light began to glimmer in the tunnels, and it was empty, his bedroll gone, and the straw strewn about.

Miserable, sniveling coward.

Once she'd gathered enough stones, she climbed back up the bank and took a path through the back streets toward the trading post where the merchants liked to gather to drink and boast and flash money around. This was the best place to find men and women eager to prove their skills at cards, the ones flush with coin from trading and brandishing their success with every word. All it usually took to provoke them was a claim that she could beat them and a taunting smile. A witch's smile, her uncle always said. Something about it stirred people to madness, either rage or occasionally a strange, frightening fascination. That same smile had provoked her uncle a thousand times when she'd still be in his care in her father's house. Now, she put it to work for her.

The bakers were out, shaking floury aprons into the wind as gusts of heat burst from the bakeries behind them along Bread Street. A rat skittered across her path with a crust in its mouth. An arch loomed ahead, snarled with vines, their leaves white with morning frost even though it was summer.

The kidnapping happened so fast she barely had time to scream. Two men stepped from the archway. Briand slowed, her neck prickling. As she hesitated, two more figures moved into the street and closed around her. Hands grabbed her, a bag dropped over her head, and they swept her up and carried her away.

~

Briand was dumped onto a wooden floor some time later, hands bound before her with rope. She could hear the sound of the lake sucking at wooden pilings. They must be at the edge of the city. Her breath made a hot cloud in the stifling air of the bag around her neck, and she could see only the hazy outline of a figure moving through the threads. Her pulse beat fast and hard against her wrists and neck. She had knives hidden on her, but she didn't dare try to break free with the guard watching her.

When the thud of boots sounded in the distance, like footsteps on a boardwalk, she tensed, readying herself for the coming confrontation.

The bag was yanked from her head, and cold air rushed to her face as a thick hand hauled her to her feet. A man with a blunt, ugly face peered down at her.

She slammed her elbow into his surprised face and ran, her still-hands clawing at the nearest window to get it open. The man stumbled after her, his nose pouring blood, swearing. Briand kicked out the windowpane and hoisted herself up. She dragged the ropes around her wrists across the glass, and they snapped. She was halfway out before the man yanked her down and forced her to her knees.

"What is going on?"

A woman stood at the threshold, draped in a long gray cloak of thick velvet with a hood that covered her head and hung almost to her eyes. She was thin, almost skeletal, as if all the fat had been sucked from her, but still, she had a haunting, deathly beauty.

The woman raised one hand, beckoning. Men clad in leather and armed with swords stepped past her, fanning out as if to block any possible exit. Mercenary soldiers by the look of them. They kept their eyes trained on Briand, but their attention was fixed on the cloaked woman like dogs heeding a master.

"Girl," the cloaked woman said, addressing Briand. "Do you know what I am?"

"You're a Seeker." Briand intended to sound fierce, but she faltered at the word. Visions of torture filled her head.

The woman laughed, low and mocking. "Yes, but only a Cleric, little sparrow. I lack the magic hands of a Sighted; I do the dirty work. You're afraid? How amusing. My men came quaking in their boots to capture you, and here you are, a shivering girl. Anabis exaggerated you, I suppose, to disguise his incompetence. How like him."

Another figure stepped into the room from behind the soldiers.

Rook. He'd found another way to get coins, it seemed.

"Is this the girl we inquired about?" the Seeker woman asked him.

"It's her." He wouldn't meet anyone's eyes as he spoke the words. "When do I get my money?"

The woman looked at him as if he were an insect unworthy of more than the barest of inspections. She made a motion with her hand, a little flick of her finger. One of the men stepped to Rook's side, and quick as gutting a fish, sliced his throat. Blood splashed across the floor. Rook fell to his knees, eyes widening, a gargling sound coming from his mouth. He pitched onto his stomach, arms splayed, a red puddle spreading outward.

Briand swallowed a gasp as the red of Rook's blood filled her vision.

The Cleric turned back to her. "Where were we?"

"If you're going to kill me," Briand said, "then do it and get it over with."

"Oh no," the Cleric said. "Not yet." She gestured again. "Tie her hands again. Quickly. We need to move."

"What about the body?" the man asked, wiping the knife on his shift. He nodded at Rook.

"Leave it."

Two of the men bound twine around Briand's wrists, then took her by the arms and hustled her to the back door. The lock scraped, the hinges protested, and then she was in the merciless midday sunlight, wind whipping at her cheeks and curling beneath her cloak. A dock stretched out over the blackish water, the planks uneven and crooked. At the end of it, a ship fought its tie to land, rising and falling on the waves, a single sail lashed to the mast, a crew scurrying across the deck like mice on a biscuit box.

The memory of Rook's face, frozen in shock as he died, lingered in Briand's mind like the pain after a slap.

She couldn't get on that ship, not if she wanted to escape. She couldn't swim.

Waves swirled and crashed beneath the end of the dock, but below the ground was a mix of rocks and sand, a pitiful shore strewn with driftwood and bits of boats washed up on the beach.

Briand made a decision.

She stumbled, falling with her bound hands reached out to catch herself, reached for the hidden knife in her boot as she went down on one knee. A quick jerk of the twine over the blade and she was up, the ties unspooling from her wrists as she shoved her shoulder into the groin of the man on the right. The woman in gray shouted something from the door and Briand dropped and cut the legs out from man on the left with her foot, knocking him off the dock. She was up and running for where the dock met the shore, the breath in her lungs burning.

Behind her, the Cleric bellowed something.

A figure ran from the boat toward her, pursuing.

Briand hit the ground in an explosion of sand. She skidded on pebbles as she ducked beneath the dock and made for the city in the distance. She was Catfoot. She was fast. She had the advantage of surprise, a head start.

Gulls screamed overhead. She couldn't hear the pursuer over the pounding of the waves and the crashing of her pulse.

A body slammed into her, knocking her down. She hit the sand on hands and knees before she scrambled up, this time with the knife from her boot in her hand.

The figure behind her caught her wrist and yanked her around. They went down together hard on the ground. She couldn't breathe. She stabbed blindly, blade meeting flesh along his ribs. He hissed in pain.

He had her pinned down with one shoulder while he grappled for the knife with both hands. Black trousers, black shirt, face half-hidden by a cowl. He wrestled the knife out of her hand and threw it into the waves. She was already pulling out the other one, the one she kept in the other boot, but he'd anticipated her move again, catching her wrist in his hand and twisting it hard. She dropped it.

Now he had taken two of her knives.

Briand lay still, hoping he'd drop his guard now that he thought she'd given up. There was a third knife. She drew in another breath.

"I surrender," she said to make him lower his guard.

A necklace swung over her face, a brown amulet, and his cowl fell away as he shifted. Shock lanced her like lightning, immobilizing her.

"Hello, Catfoot," he murmured for her ears alone as the soldiers came pounding up the shore.

He was thinner than she remembered, his eyes dark and heavy with secrets, his jaw covered in stubble. A seam of fresh scar poked from his collar. His eyes bored into hers, holding her captive, daring her to be silent.

"Kael," she whispered.

The Cleric's men rushed around them both and pulled her to her feet. Behind them, the woman in gray stood on the dock, her cloak and robes billowing in the wind.

She was dragged away to the ship. She twisted her head once to look at him, and he stood with his arms crossed in the wind, face unreadable.

She didn't understand.

FOUR

KAEL WATCHED AS the dragonsayer vanished on the waiting boat in the grip of the guards, her thin body taut with resistance. His side throbbed where she'd cut him, and his shirt was already sticky and heavy with a blossoming of blood. Her knife lay at his feet, and the other was exposed as a wave ran back into the lake. He crouched to pick them up. She probably had more knives squirreled away somewhere on her. She was a tricky thing, and he didn't trust her for a moment, especially not now. Not when she'd seen him like this.

Kael slid the knives into his belt and strode for the dock.

The ship set sail immediately, lurching as it caught the wind. The crew gave him a wide berth, for he had a reputation, one he'd cultivated. He ignored them as he descended to the lowest deck, leaving a few droplets of blood behind him on the steps while a cabin boy stared at them, wide-eyed.

"Where is the captive?" he asked the nearest guard.

A presence tickled the back of his neck, and the guard straightened instead of responding. Kael turned without his answer.

The Cleric, Calys, stood watching him as she always did, with a mixture of suspicion and derision. Kael met her gaze steadily. She wanted him to be weak, the traitor who couldn't take the torture of the Seekers, the spineless captured turncoat who failed to keep his oath to his prince in the face of horrible pain. But he would never give her that satisfaction. He never squirmed or shifted under the direct weight of her stare as she wanted him to.

"You're injured." She liked to make observations. Kael liked to say nothing. The dynamic had served to frustrate them both thus far on this mission.

He touched the wet fabric of his shirt. His fingers came away red. It was only a flesh wound, but still, he would need to tend to it quickly.

"If we had a Healer," Calys continued, "we could take care of that immediately. Alas, we are in this remote wilderness trash heap."

Kael had experienced a Healing once, icy fingers pressed against his injured flesh to rearrange the insides of him with magic and knit the skin and muscle together in a flash of burning fire and searing, hot power. The nightmares still plagued him in his sleep. No, he'd far rather take a needle to the ragged cut, sew the skin with thread, splash it with wine, and then bundle herbs in the bandages and endure the healing process than be a conduit for raw magic from one of those experimental butchers they had the audacity to call Healers. Call him old-fashioned.

The Cleric turned away for her cabin, and Kael pressed a hand against his wound and went to find bandages.

After he'd washed away the blood and bound the slice across his ribs, Kael found the dragonsayer in the bottom of the ship, huddled inside the cage they'd brought especially for her, as if she were a dragon in human form, capable of breathing fire and eating men.

She lifted her head from her knees at his approach, that cutting, defiant stare in her witching eyes as she recognized him. Guttersnipe. Catfoot. Dragonsayer. She was all those things at once in the scrapes on her chin, the tendrils of hair around her dirty face, and the feline curve of her wary shoulders.

"Tell me it isn't true," she said when he reached the bars of the cage. "Tell me this is a mistake. A dream. A mission—"

"I'm with them," he said. "The Monarchists are nothing to me. They never were."

The words slugged her, and the flicker of doubt on her face gave way to a landslide of despair. He saw it unfold in her eyes, rapid as breathing, the way she lost her faith in him.

"Spy," she hissed. "Traitor. I trusted you."

It gutted him to see the fury and heartbreak mingle in her eyes when she looked at him, but he would never show her that.

"Why?" she burst out finally.

He measured his words. "You wouldn't understand."

She was resplendent with scorn. "Which part would I not understand? The part where you've betrayed your prince, the one you risked everything—my cousin's life as well as mine—for? The part where you lied about returning for me, lied about your devotion to the Monarchists, lied about everything?"

37

She wanted a reaction, surely, but he wasn't going to give her one.

"I didn't know you were such a Monarchist," he said.

"I'm not." She turned her face toward the wall. Her shoulders rose and fell with a breath. "I care nothing for politics. A king is a king is a king. But I thought *you* did."

"People are often not what we think they are," he said.

She curled her fingers as if she wanted to strike him. "How could you have abandoned the others? Nath, Tibus, Bran? Where are they? What have you done to them? Are they even still alive?"

He didn't answer.

"Tell me," she raged.

He could not.

He had nothing more to say, so he left.

~

Briand stayed huddled in the middle of the cage, her knees drawn up to her chest and her chin pressed to her collarbone. Was she stupid to think that anyone would be trustworthy? That anyone would have honor? The thieves didn't, her uncle didn't, but she'd thought Kael, of all people, did. She still remembered Kael's face as Drune's betrayal was revealed, the sheer brokenness that had marred his features, as clearly as if it had happened yesterday.

She drew out her last knife, this one small as a finger and easily concealed. She slipped it into the padlock that hung on the door to the gate, pressing her ear to the lock to listen to the gears. She sweated as she worked, grinding the blade back and forth, hissing curses that she'd never learned to properly pick locks.

Footsteps rattled on the ladder, and she scrambled back, hiding the knife. She didn't find it difficult to summon a face of despair and rage as a guard descended with a bucket of food, like slops for a pig. She watched him with her witching gaze as he opened the door of the cage and stepped inside. She tensed, but all he did was drop the bucket with a thud.

"Dinner," he said, and grinned at her. Her skin prickled.

"What if I refuse to eat?"

"Then I get to pour it down your throat."

She ate the food.

It was a fish stew, oily and thin. The guard watched her swallow every spoonful, his arms crossed as he leaned against the bars of the cage.

"Little thing, aren't you?" he said. "I expected someone more... impressive."

Briand didn't respond to him. She licked her fingers and kicked the bucket across the floor, never breaking eye contact. She straightened slightly, making herself larger, her shoulders higher. She'd learned in the last few years how much little details like that mattered, the eye contact, the body posture. She wanted him to think she wasn't afraid of him. She wanted him to wonder how much power the girl locked in the metal cage like a monster possessed and be afraid to come any closer.

The guard stared at her as if trying to see beneath her skin. "They say you can call creatures with your mind." He paused. "Dragons."

He sounded uncertain, curious, and a little delighted, like a boy who had discovered his father's sword.

Her heart banged against her ribs. Sweat prickled across her back. She didn't take her eyes from his. She thought of the final knife, hastily hidden away. If he tried anything, she was going to put the blade through his eye. It would slip straight to his brain like a needle through burlap. She smiled at him, a toothy smile full of confidence, even though inside she was shaking.

Finally, the guard picked up the bucket and slammed the cage door behind him.

As soon as he'd vanished, Briand felt every inch of the floor and bars to see if there were any weaknesses, any places she might be able to break free.

Nothing.

She drew out her final knife again and returned to the lock.

~

Time passed. The ship rolled and pitched beneath her. The hull groaned, and she imagined the lake beneath her, dark and deep, with secret things writhing through the miles of water.

The lock refused to open despite her efforts. Her fingers cramped and her wrists ached. Panic scuttled through her, and she had to stop and breathe.

She heard the shouts of the crew, the clunk of equipment. The water sounded different. They were docking.

The light tracked across the floor from where it came through the slats above, and when the trapdoor opened and footsteps clanged on the ladder again, Briand hid the knife and braced herself for the guard, with his leers and comments.

It was a different guard, this one with no bucket. He motioned to her as he unlocked the cage door. He didn't appear to notice the scrape marks around the opening left by her blade.

"Get up," he said. He glanced at the trapdoor as if wondering where his fellows were, and then he stepped into the cage, arms spread wide as if to frighten her back like he might ward off a wild creature.

He was nervous. It made him skittish and careless. She could work with that. She pressed against the bars, calculating the distance between him and the opening.

She sucked in a breath, gathering the tension in her body, and then she snarled at him like an animal. He recoiled, and she leaped forward, squeezing past him. He grabbed, but his fingernails only scraped her skin as she ran for the ladder.

Orange-gold light poured down from the square of freedom above as Briand scrambled up, quick as a cat, banging her ankle against the wooden slats. The guard was behind her, shouting hoarsely. She reached the deck and leaped to her feet, scanning the boat. Three guards ran toward her. She darted left, heading for the bow. Wind snatched at her clothes as she reached the side of the boat and caught the rail.

They hadn't docked yet. The shore was still too far.

She couldn't swim.

An arm encircled her, hauling her back. *Kael.* She clawed at his arm, but he held her tightly as the guards reached them both, the one sent to fetch her furious and red-faced. He reached for her, his mouth already spitting insults, but Kael warned him off with a single furious snap of an order.

"Don't try to run again," Kael said in her ear. "You'll only be caught, Catfoot."

She wanted to slam her elbow into his face and feel it break. She thought of the knife she had hidden, but it wasn't time. She didn't reach for it. Not yet.

As Kael hustled her across the deck toward the captain's cabin, she twisted her head to take one final look at the lake. Across the water, a cluster of buildings huddled against an unfamiliar shore, just a few dwellings clumped around a ponderous stone fort and a lighthouse. A light burned in one of the windows.

Then he marched her into the captain's cabin, and she faced the woman in gray.

FIVE

AUBERON FLICKED HIS Seeker's robes from his wrists as he stood before the window, looking out at the wretched brown puddle of a lake that lapped at the village and lighthouse below. He'd always loved the way the robes flowed around him like wind as he walked, the way they cloaked him in secrecy and power, but today they seemed strangling. A stench blew off the water, bringing with it the promise of a coming storm.

He closed his eyes, longing for the chaos of thunder and lightning. Storms always helped him think, and right now, he needed to think. Calys was returning today, and he was too unsettled to face her with his usual temperament unless he could calm himself.

He sucked in a breath of air to clear his head and tasted the muck of the lake on the wind. He loathed this filthy place almost as much as he loathed pretending to be just another simpering, luxury-loving blueblood with enough powers to grant him the Seeker robes and an eventual place in the Citadel's Hall of Voices.

He did, of course, love luxury, and his blood was pure. But he would never be satisfied with merely a seat in the Hall of Voices.

No, he had ambitions far higher.

Unfortunately, ambitions sometimes required bootlicking, and the boots Auberon had chosen were none other than those of the second highest Grayrobe in the Citadel, Rodis of Gorn. Rodis had been obsessed with this rumor of a resurrected ancient myth since the death of his brother, Anabis, and Auberon had been the one assigned to travel with Rodis's Cleric in pursuit of these nonsensical dreams instead of remaining at Tasglorn and the Citadel. A dragonsayer, of all things.

Auberon was hardly superstitious. His years as a Seeker had chased any notions of destiny and fate out of his mind. But he was committed to convincing the higher ups that he was worthy of promotion, and so he'd been traveling this cursed backwater territory for months now in search of the dragonsayer, with no word from Tasglorn until this morning. The letter had come via mechanical bird, the mechbird whirring in near exhaustion as it dropped into his hand. It had flown at maximum speed to reach him, and judging from the wear on the gears, it had been searching for him for some time. Blasted backwater routes. The mechanicals never seemed to work correctly in this wilderness. It was as if some ancient power confounded them.

The letter's contents were... troubling. It was from Jade, his sister. Accusations had been made against the family. A tribunal had been called. He would have to submit to a mind read when he returned—it was all formality, of course, but...

But...

He knew what they were looking for. If they read his mind, they'd know it too.

Some secrets had to stay buried.

He snapped his eyes open as a knock came at the door. One of the guards stepped inside at his curt order, the man scraping and bowing to him as they all did here, but he saw the barely-concealed disdain in the man's eyes.

Auberon's lip curled as anger filled him. He had no patience left for this miserable place after the news in the letter. "What is it?"

"Calys has arrived with a prisoner. She says it may be the thing you've been seeking."

Another miserable pretender dredged from the gutter of a muddy wilderness port. He wanted to smash something against the wall and see the soldier flinch. He wanted to inflict his rage on something.

"Is the traitor with them?" he asked.

"Yes, sir."

The impotent anger he felt now had a direction. The traitor had been a thorn to him since he'd arrived at the Citadel with his loyalty to barter. And despite his lack of powers and his betrayal of his foolish companions, he still reeked of a despicable sense of honor that Auberon found galling.

Perhaps it was time for another test.

He turned from the window and found his wine goblet, the hideous one with gemstones as big as knuckle bones. He'd discovered it the other day while searching the storeroom. He always did perform better with a prop in his hand.

"Bring more soldiers, and I want them armed," he ordered.

~

Kael held Briand's arm tightly as they faced Calys. He could feel her tremble, but she lifted her chin, unbowed before the Cleric.

"We go ashore here," Calys said to Kael. "Auberon will examine her. Keep her under your thumb, or you'll pay for your incompetence."

"I will ensure she's brought to heel," Kael said.

Briand stiffened, whether in dismay or defiance, he didn't know. If he were a betting man, he would pick defiance. Pieter's niece had rarely exhibited anything else since he'd known her.

Calys made a motion of dismissal, and he pulled Briand outside the cabin before the dragonsayer could settle on defiance and ignite Calys's anger. She was rigid as he dragged her along, her face tight with fury.

A slender board stretched between the deck and the rounded stones of the shore. Carru lay beyond, an outpost on the edge of the western province of Tasna. The air smelled of stale river water and rotting reeds. Stone houses cut from the rock clustered like stacks of bricks along the cliffs, and a few fishing boats bobbed in the water, casting dark blue shadows against the orange blush of the sunset across the waves. Fishing birds with long beaks flew overhead, screeching before they landed in the water with a wet flap of their wings.

He escorted her to the shore himself, keeping a firm hand on her arm. Soldiers keeping watch at the dock watched as they passed, hands on weapons as they appraised Kael and his captive. They couldn't tell who he was, as he wore no insignia or other indication of rank. A man in black and a slender woman-girl in trousers. They turned away, seeming to dismiss the duo as curious, but unremarkable.

The fort loomed an ugly block of cracked stone and clay, its walls lined with bored soldiers. Their voices carried in the still evening air—a chuckle, a curse, a muttered question.

Briand squinted up at them, tense again. Kael remembered how the guards at her uncle's castle used to torment her.

The gates opened. He scanned the yard, taking in the numbers of the men. This outpost was well-manned. The ramparts held far more archers than needed. He turned his head and took stock of the carts piled with supplies at the end of the yard. Enough food for an army.

A troop practiced in the interior of the fort, in the middle of a dusty patch of grass. They stood in lines, rehearsing a series of moves. They practiced with rifles.

Beside him, Briand had grown alert. She followed his gaze thoughtfully.

He kept walking, pulling her past the barracks and toward the fort's living quarters for the officers.

Inside, the hall flickered with candles set in sconces along the stone walls. Carru was too remote to have electricity like the larger cities, let alone anything approaching the technological wonders of Tasglorn, the capital. This place was a backwater, a place for soldiers to be sent when they'd fallen out of favor or needed to be taught a lesson.

Except now the fort brimmed with activity, and the soldiers trained with rifles.

A pair of carved wooden doors stood at the end of the hall, a pair of dragons. Briand's mouth turned in a wry smile, an angry twitch of her lips that said she found the depiction ironic, and Kael almost smiled too. He banged his fist against the left one, and after an eon of silence, it opened with a groan.

The fort's steward peered out, and his eyes widened at the sight of them. He mumbled something and stumbled back, leaving the door wide for them to enter.

A flicker of warning went through Kael's mind as he stepped inside with Briand, a brush of bad feeling, a spider's web of suggestion that danced along his nerves, and he pushed Briand back against the door and drew his sword as he was surrounded by six men, their rifles pointed at his chest.

SIX

KAEL LIFTED HIS eyes from the barrels of the rifles to where across the room, a young Seeker stood with a ridiculously large goblet studded with blue stones in his hand, watching him.

Auberon.

The Seeker was young, too thin and too tall, with a cruel mouth, carefully groomed eyebrows, and a sharp, aristocratic chin. He was dark of complexion like most Austrisians, but his hair was the color of ash, and it fell into his black eyes as he leaned forward. He wore robes of crushed gray silk beneath his cloak, and a heavy gold signet ring glinted on his right hand over his glove. Son of a prominent nobleman in Tasglorn, a prodigy among the Seekers. Vicious when provoked. Spoiled. Dangerous, because he was unpredictable.

"Ah," Auberon said, as if surprised to see them, as if he hadn't ordered his soldiers to train their weapons on Kael moments before. "The traitor, and... a girl? This draggled thing is supposed to be a dragonsayer?"

Kael kept his sword at the throat of the nearest soldier. "What are you doing?" He kept his eyes trained on the Seeker. He could feel Briand behind him, her breath on his neck. She didn't move.

Auberon swirled the wine in his goblet as he spoke. The ring on his finger flashed. "Examining your loyalty."

"I've proven my loyalty," Kael said softly.

"Monarchists—even turncoat Monarchists—are like dogs. Turn your back and they're into the chicken, or the meat pies, or even their own vomit." He took of sip from the goblet. "So, surprise! I am going to read your mind, just to see what hideous things you've been thinking." He snapped his fingers at the guards. "Take her away. I'll deal with her next."

Calys strode into the room before they could obey. She halted at the sight of Kael surrounded by soldiers, then sighed. "Auberon..."

"One can never be too careful," he said.

"If you're going to persist in this, then hurry up and do it. No need for speeches."

"You're *such* a Cleric," Auberon said. "There is always a need for speeches. How else are we to inspire those beneath us?" He waved the drink in his hand.

"That goblet is ridiculous."

"Isn't it? I found it in the storage rooms. I need something proper to drink out of. I'm not a savage, Calys. I won't sip wine from a flagon like a common garrison guard."

He talked foppishly, but it was an act. Kael had seen him in unguarded moments. The man was like a snake coiled to strike.

Kael remained still as Auberon set down the goblet and approached him, striping the glove from his left hand and tucking it into his belt. His fingernails were long and slender and painted dark, his palm unblemished. The Seeker flicked his fingers, and the soldiers drew back but didn't lower their weapons.

The soldiers pulled Briand away.

Kael steeled himself for pain.

"Hold him," the Seeker ordered, and two of the soldiers stepped to Kael's side and grabbed his arms, forcing him down into a kneeling position. Kael kept his head up, meeting the Seeker's eyes squarely as the other reached out his bare hand gripped Kael's temple with a splayed hand. Kael stiffened, but made no sound. His eyes closed.

It was like lightning against his skull.

He ground his teeth together and focused. He was in a field, surrounded by blue sky and golden grass. Horses grazed to his left. He could feel the wind cool against his forehead and neck. He clung to the scene as the pain crawled inside his head and made him shudder.

Finally, the Seeker released him. The soldiers released Kael, who rose to his feet slowly. He kept his face carefully composed. His head ached, and his vision was blurred.

Calys sighed loudly. "I grow weary of these charades of power, Auberon. We aren't in Tasglorn. There is no one here to be impressed by you."

Auberon tipped his head toward the Cleric as he flexed his bare hand.

"Shall we see about this dragonsayer you've captured?"

~

Briand paced in the empty room, listening for screams. She had heard the stories of how a Seeker could make a man claw the flesh from his own body due to the pain inflicted in his mind. She'd heard how they could steal secrets with a touch, harvest thoughts and plans through their fingertips.

The door opened, and the Seeker entered, followed by the Cleric. Kael was not with them. She felt a flicker of panic. What had they done to him?

The room seemed to darken, the walls closing in as she was captured within the intensity of the Seeker's stare. His eyes were dark brown, almost black, with a slim ring of pale blue at the center that seemed to crackle with restlessness. There was something unsettling about them, a hint of dark magic that crawled with frightful power.

"Dragonsayer," he said, testing the word. He raised one eyebrow as if to say, *you?*

She shrank away.

"Hold her," the Seeker snapped, and hands gripped Briand's shoulders.

He reached out his bare hand, palm flat and fingers extended, fingers curling as he cupped Briand's chin. An icy tingle shot through her head and curled around her neck like a chain along with a jagged pain like a broken knife. She pushed back as she felt the memories rise, but she was helpless against the tide that broke over her.

Her father's death. Her uncle's scorn and neglect. They surfaced and melted away. She pushed again, but the memories coming faster now. The yawning empty after Kael and the others left, the way she wanted to stop existing from the pain of abandonment.

She was drowning in the memories and the emotions they contained. She pushed again with her mind, and could not free herself, and so she did something else.

She *pulled.*

A shock shot through her to her fingertips, along with a flood of new memories. A garden filled with bronze statues and a woman weeping. A circle of men and women in gray, hands outstretched. Blood on a white stone floor. A black pit of grief in her belly.

The Seeker jerked his hand away, and the pain ceased, but Briand's head kept buzzing, her thoughts wheeling like birds in a storm. She gulped a breath, shaking.

Auberon stared at her in horror, his skin ashen.

"Well?" Calys said from behind him. She couldn't see his face.

Auberon's expression smoothed over, and when he spoke, his tone was composed.

"She's not the dragonsayer."

Not the dragonsayer. Briand didn't understand. Why was he telling lies?

"What?" Calys snapped.

"She's not the one we seek," Auberon said. He pulled on his glove and turned away.

Calys stared at him, furious, as if it were his fault. "My sources promised—"

"You should get better sources," Auberon said.

Calys made a sound of disgust and motioned to the guards still flanking Briand. "Kill her."

Briand's stomach dropped as one drew his sword. "Please— I have information—"

"Shut up," Calys said.

Auberon kept his eyes on his glove, his tone disinterested, but a vein in his throat throbbed. "Let's not kill her."

Calys held up her hand to halt the guards. "What?"

"I want her alive."

The Cleric looked thoroughly disenchanted with her life and situation. "I have no interest in keeping prisoners around for you to play with."

Auberon laughed at that. "You are mistaken. I don't have any interest in scrawny, dirty things like her. This is for the benefit of the Citadel, I assure you."

Calys's lip curled. She clearly didn't believe him. She shook her head and left the room, and Auberon motioned to the guards. "Put her in the dungeon."

Briand's head was still spinning as the guards escorted her away.

~

Auberon paced alone in his borrowed chamber at the top of the commander's house. Shock still reverberated through him.

She had repelled him. Slipped from his grasp like a smooth stone coated in ice. Her mind had been completely impervious to his reach.

He'd read scores of minds. He'd never encountered anything like it. She was simply inaccessible.

He thought of the letter he'd received and the way it had burned up in the flame of the grate, the words about the tribunal that awaited him vanishing into smoke.

Whatever magic this girl used, he needed it. Desperately.

SEVEN

THE DUNGEON WAS built from ancient, sweaty stones. Moisture rising from the sea seeped through cracks in the walls along with the smell of rot. It was dark except for the light that came through the slits of windows high in the walls.

Briand sat curled in the furthest corner of her cell, thinking. She was trying to sort out what Kael had said to her on the ship, and what he hadn't said.

The cells around hers were empty except for the one directly beside hers, which held a young girl, her hair a snarl of black curls. She crept to the bars and stared at Briand.

"The Seekers brought you here," she said.

Briand surfaced from her thoughts and looked at the girl. "Yes. You?"

The girl curled her fingers around the bars and pressed her face against them. "No, I'm in for writing 'Lordae smells like dog vomit' on the fortress walls."

Briand laughed, startled.

The girl paused, then added, "Lordae is the commander. He takes our food and makes us work to keep his soldiers supplied with firewood and supplies. We all hate him." She glanced at the stairs and lowered her voice. "Did Hunters capture you?"

"Hunters?"

She nodded, eyes wide. "Some passed through our village once. They wear cloaks with the armor underneath, and those masks... Gave me nightmares just to look at them. They were stalking a defector. The whole village heard his screams that night."

"No," Briand said. "I wasn't brought by Hunters. Just a Cleric."

"They're all demons anyway," the girl said.

The door scraped open above, and a soldier descended. He opened the girl's cell. "The commander says you will be flogged ten lashes and then released."

The girl stood. She didn't even look frightened. Just resigned.

Briand put her head down on her knees and closed her eyes.

~

The sun had crept below the horizon and the moon had taken its place when Kael came to her cell. The guards let him inside and withdrew at his command. He stood by the door, dressed in black with a fine cloak, looking washed and shaved as if he were about to attend a dinner party.

"Are you plotting how best to slit my throat?" Kael asked after what seemed like an interminable silence.

"If I did, you'd deserve it."

He sighed, a heavy sound. He was maddeningly calm.

Briand was exhausted by the maelstrom of emotions inside her. Her hand itched for the familiar shape of a knife's handle, so solid and uncomplicated—knives had few things to say, and they got everyone's attention so beautifully—not like the gossamer, painfully thin web of persuasion, of silver-tongued speech that she so often fumbled with.

But she had words to speak to him. Words she had been thinking all day.

"You aren't a traitor," she whispered, her lips barely moving as the words fell into the space between them.

His eyes were startling in their intensity. He didn't say anything. He watched her as if he had three guesses as to what she was going to say next, and he had put all his money on one of them.

"You just let me think that so when they read my mind, they wouldn't see that you aren't," she continued. She felt no triumph in her deduction, only weariness.

The place between his eyebrows relaxed slightly, a confirmation.

Briand felt no relief. This game of life and death had her stretched thin like skin over a starving man's bones, and playing opposite Kael made her feel angry and sick, even more so than seeing him. Or perhaps not. She couldn't sort out her feelings at the moment. They had merged into a single burning mass in her chest.

"I know this moment isn't the time for confessions, but you're going to have to explain yourself eventually," she said.

"I know." It was his only admission.

He was still watching her as if waiting for some sign. She didn't know what he wanted from her. She didn't know what she wanted from him.

She was waiting too.

"I'm on a mission," he said so quietly she almost couldn't make the words out. "But I've gotten what I need. I was going to make my escape when I heard they were going to capture the dragonsayer. So I waited."

She was still angry for many reasons, but she accepted the words for what they were: a peace offering.

"How did you trick the Seeker? He read your mind."

"I've had training. And there are other ways to circumvent them. For instance, overload the mind with shock and you can lock the Seekers out temporarily."

Was that what happened to her? Was that why Auberon hadn't been able to tell she was the dragonsayer?

She curled her fingers around the bars and rested her forehead against them. "I have an idea for our escape. Part of one, anyway."

"Oh?"

She told him, and he smiled.

"You'll need a knife," he said.

Briand pulled her final dagger from beneath her braided bun, where the blade had lain along her scalp like a snake on a rock for the last several days. It was a tiny dagger, barely bigger than her palm.

"I knew it," Kael said with a shake of his head.

That wrung a small smile from her.

Tension lay between them, thick with things she wanted to say and ask. The words were stacked like bricks in her mind, layers upon layers, weighing her down, walling her up. She didn't ask those questions, though. The answers were sure to cut a thousand slices along her insides and then be left to bleed in secret, and she didn't have the fortitude to withstand that, not now. She needed all her mental strength to escape first.

Footsteps sounded on the stone steps. She moved away from Kael, and he straightened and put his hand on the door.

It was only the guards, bringing food. Among them was the one she'd threatened on the boat.

Kael didn't look back as he left.

She scuttled forward when they'd gone and snatched up the bread they'd left. Moldy. She picked the bad parts off and left the crumbs for the ants.

~

When the stripes of light from the window slits had appeared again, pinkish-blue with the light of dawn, footsteps sounded on the curving staircase of stone.

Briand raised her head, expecting a guard again.

It was Auberon, the Seeker.

He stopped at the bars, and the light from the windows illuminated his cheekbones and made shadows along his nose. He studied her a moment in silence, pressing his tongue against the inside of his cheek.

Briand said nothing. She waited, watching his hands. They were not gloved, and his fingernails glimmered like talons.

"You," Auberon said. "Who taught you?"

"I have no formal education."

"I don't mean letters. I mean your mind. Don't make me force it out of you. It won't be pleasant."

"I can't answer you if I don't know what you ask. Taught me what?"

Instead of responding, he reached for her, and although she shrank back against the stone wall, still he could reach far enough to press his hand to her forehead. Reflexively, she pulled in response, and a flicker of darkness rushed through her, a memory of being struck across the face in a room with golden curtains by a man whose neck bulged with fury. Not her memory. She didn't understand.

He yanked his hand back.

"Unbelievable," he said. "I've never encountered..." He stopped. "Your mind is like ice. There's nothing to grab, nothing to sift through. As if you were a corpse, yet you breathe. His bare hand shot out, one fingernail grazing her cheek. She clapped a hand over the stinging place, feeling wetness.

"Yet you bleed," Auberon murmured.

She watched him, letting him talk as she held her hand to her cheek to stem the blood, and tried to understand.

He reached again, this time pressing his whole hand against her forehead. His fingers dug into her skull, fingernails like claws against her skin. He growled something beneath his breath, and she seized his wrists, trying to throw him off, but the blast of pain was like lightning, staggering her, and then she saw birds in a red sky and a tomb with a statue of a woman in front of it. Then she shoved Auberon's hand away and braced herself against the wall, panting.

"You are using powerful magic," he said.

Understanding dawned. He couldn't read her mind. Somehow, instead, she was reading his.

"You lied to the other one," she said. "The Cleric. You don't want her to know you can't see my thoughts."

Auberon wrapped his hands around two of the bars and leaned close. "If I declared you were the dragonsayer, she would have taken you to Tasglorn and the Citadel. This way, you remain here."

"What does she want with the dragonsayer?" Briand's heart beat hard against her ribs.

He drew back from the cell and tucked his hands beneath his cloak like a priest. "I don't know. Those are the orders from the Citadel."

"You're not going to let me go," she said. "I'm not stupid."

"You have no alternatives but to trust me," he said. "I hold your life in my hand. Remember that. Work with me. Surely you want your freedom."

This could work to the plan.

She said nothing, and after a moment, he turned to go.

"If you want my cooperation," Briand said, before he could leave, "you won't leave me in this filth." She spread her hands to indicate the cell.

Auberon turned back with a chuckle. "Are you saying you want a bath?"

Briand didn't laugh. "And dinner. At a proper table. I've had too many meals out of a bucket lately."

Auberon looked as if she'd handed him a dirty shirt and told him to wash it. "Fine. I will... arrange it."

Hope was just a flutter of her pulse as he disappeared up the staircase.

EIGHT

A FEW HOURS passed before a woman came, puffing from the stairs, carrying a bucket and a bundle. She was large and doughy, her hair tucked beneath a white cap except for a few black strands that escaped around her neck and ears. She plopped the bucket down and thrust the bundle through the bars at Briand.

A dress spilled out, a mass of green silk and crinkly starched linen underskirts. Briand held it up, and the fabric glimmered in the light. A web of embroidered vines covered the bodice and curled around the short, lacy sleeves.

"Put it on," the woman instructed. She looked like a housekeeper, with a striped apron over her plain gray dress. She scowled at Briand as though everything wrong with the world was her fault. "But wash first." She knocked her foot against the bucket, and a splash of sudsy water slopped over the side.

Briand peered at the bucket through the bars. The woman was already turning to leave without another word. She didn't unlock the door, so Briand stretched out her arm and dragged it closer. A rag floated in the soapy water, and she plucked it out. She undressed furtively, one eye on the staircase in case a guard returned, and scrubbed herself fast and hard enough to scrape off a little skin with the dirt. It felt good to be clean after days wearing grime.

When she'd finished washing, she put on the dress. The layers billowed around her on the straw, and it was comical—this fine dress in the filth of the dungeon. Briand straightened the fabric and then rolled up her clothing into a tight ball that she bound around her thigh (the dress was so voluptuous that it wasn't obvious) with a bit of extra rag. She wasn't going to be caught without her things. They'd been made by Reela, and they were precious.

Besides, she wasn't escaping in this ridiculously impractical gown.

Hours passed again, and her stomach gnawed with hunger. Finally, the woman returned, breathing heavily again, this time trailed by a guard.

"Come," the woman ordered. The guard unlocked the door and swung it open, and Briand stepped out, acting meek, letting them think that a pretty dress and a pitiful scrub from a bucket were enough to placate her into docility.

They climbed the stairs to the main level of the fort. Windows cut into the stone let in light and air, and she could smell the lake, briny and fresh. Sunlight blazed down in the yard outside, and dark clouds sat on the horizon, a promise of a coming storm. The sound of soldiers drilling echoed through the hall as they marched forward in an odd procession of bored man, old woman, and glittering girl.

The woman stopped before a carved door. She turned to Briand.

"You'll be dining with the commander and the others, so try to find some manners."

Briand supposed she did look like an urchin, her hair in a snarl, her face weathered from sun and wind in Gillspin, her eyes sharp with resentment and suspicion. Guttersnipe was written on her face.

"Who does the dress belong to?" she asked.

The woman sniffed as if to say the question was out of line. "It belonged to the commander's wife."

Then she opened the door and shooed Briand inside.

A table of polished wood filled the room, surrounded with empty chairs except at the end, where a small group of individuals sat. A banquet hall, although it looked grimy and unused. They'd probably only dusted it off because the Seekers were here. Two rusty chandeliers hung from an arching ceiling, unlit, and a row of windows without glass afforded an open-air view of the lake.

Heads turned at her entrance. The Cleric paused in the middle of a bite, her frosty eyes landing on Briand and lingering as if she were looking for a reason to call the guards. Kael sat to the Cleric's left. He barely looked up from cutting his meat when Briand entered, although she noticed how his hands stilled for a second. Auberon sat to the Cleric's right, drinking wine. He looked at her as though she was a curiosity that had been dredged up from the lake below, as if it wasn't his doing that brought her there.

A pair of men she didn't recognize sat across from Kael and the Seekers. The fort's commander, recognizable by his uniform, stood.

"Please sit, miss," he said. He motioned to an empty chair beside one of the other men with a sweep of his hand.

Briand crossed to the place he'd indicated, and the man next to it jumped up to pull her chair back. She wondered if they knew anything about her. Did the dress inspire some automatic gentlemanly instinct? Or were they afraid of the Seekers and assuming her to be one of them?

"Thank you...?" she said, as if she had some semblance of manners, but more for the purpose of learning his name.

The man sat down again. He was middle-aged, with a short, meticulously groomed beard and spectacles that perched at the end of his nose. "Jenet," he supplied, and then added, "I'm the doctor."

Dishes in the middle of the table steamed. There was sweetened pork surrounded by stewed apples and carrots, a cream pie with a drizzle of orange sauce, braided breads thick with seeds. Briand's stomach pinched. She reached for the serving spoon.

"Allow me," Auberon said, his voice silky smooth. He caught it from her hand with his gloved one, and she didn't let go.

Everyone at the table was watching them.

Auberon smiled at her, charm wielded like a weapon, and she released the spoon. He dished up the meat, a hearty helping from the finest cut, and heaped it with the carrots and stewed apples so the juices drooled over the sides of the meat and pooled around it.

"Bread?" he asked.

67

"Yes." She watched him select the largest piece. He paused over the cream pie, and she nodded. The whole exchange made her feel uneasy. He was reminding her with every serving that he was buying her cooperation with this meal, with the dress she wore, with the clean skin on her hands and face. She forced her mouth to stay neutral instead of slipping into a scowl as Auberon handed the plate back.

Enjoy it, Seeker, she thought. Because this power game of yours will end soon.

"Thank you," she said, because the others were still watching. What she meant was, *you're a fool.*

She ate fast, the flavors dizzyingly delicious Gillspin food and prison fare. A gingery sauce that made her lips warm crusted the skin of the pork, and the fat melted on her tongue. The bread's crust crackled, crisp and perfect. The cream pie was too rich, and she couldn't finish it.

"You look lovely in that dress," the commander said. "I'm glad we could find something among my late wife's things that fit you. When Auberon told me about your predicament, I was deeply moved, and I wanted to do anything I could to help."

Her predicament?

She didn't ask what lie Auberon had told.

Calys shot a glance at him, but she didn't ask either. Not in front of the commander and the other men.

"Being dragged all this way, forced to reside in dungeons and be kept under guard as a matter of faulty paperwork..." The commander shook his head. "I hope they can sort it out when you get to Tasglorn.

In the meantime, you are welcome at our table, my dear."

Briand looked hard at the commander. He served in Cahan's army. According to the rumors she'd heard about such men, he should be practically a monster with horns, but instead, he had an unremarkable face, tired, his mouth lined with wrinkles. His eyes hid a few shadowed secrets, perhaps, but he did not seem monstrous. He kept looking at the Seekers as though they were creatures from the lake sitting at his table, and the doctor and other man did the same.

"This is my son," the commander said, gesturing to the other man who hadn't been introduced. "An officer in Cahan's army."

The son barely glanced at Briand. He had his eyes fixed on Kael, who ate without comment. A flush colored the son's neck.

"Are we sure we must dine with this one?" he demanded.

Calys put a glass to her lips and took a sip. "He works for us."

A soft challenge.

"He is a Monarchist butcher," the son protested. "How can we share a table with such a man?"

Kael was playing the beaten-down traitor well. He put another piece of meat in his mouth.

Calys turned to the commander. "Does your son imply that we are not welcome here?"

Tension thickened in the air. Briand put down her fork, and the sound clattered through the silence.

The commander cleared his throat. "You are very welcome, of course. Jon, please."

The son, Jon, gulped his wine and glowered. "We have their kind killing our men every week. We find the bodies in the woods, or in the lake—"

"Jon," the commander said. "A lady is present."

Briand didn't know if he meant Calys or her. Calys didn't appear to know, either. Her lips quirked at the corners as she took another sip of her drink. She seemed amused to be called a lady, as if the idea that she was so delicate that she couldn't hear about a few dead bodies could be entertained by anyone.

Briand remembered the way she'd ordered Rook's death, the spray of his blood, her cold efficiency. *Leave the body.*

The doctor, Jenet, turned to Briand as if to shield her from such talk. "Miss," he said, "I hope you—"

He paused and looked closer at her hands.

"Your hands," he said, sounding alarmed.

The others turned their heads at his tone. Kael was the only one who didn't bother to look up from his plate except for a single, disinterested glance.

"What, doctor?" Briand asked, letting her voice quiver a little like the nervous lady the commander thought she was.

"I... If I may," he said, and gently turned her wrist over. Reddish, bloody spots covered the sides of her hands. The doctor muttered something that sounded like a curse. He brushed away her hair from her neck without asking permission and muttered another curse.

"What is it?" Auberon asked, his eyes narrowing.

The doctor pushed back his chair. "I, I am concerned about the lady's health based on a few symptoms I see."

Briand put a hand to her mouth. "My health? Could it have been from the dungeon?"

She carefully didn't look at Kael as she spoke.

"Do you feel ill at all?" the doctor asked.

She paused to consider his question. "I have felt quite warm for a few days, and had a headache last night."

The commander looked guilty, and Calys impatient.

"Why don't you examine her and see if she needs treatment," Auberon suggested.

Jenet nodded vigorously. "Yes, yes. Come with me, miss. I will see to you at once."

Briand swallowed a smile as she stood and followed the doctor out of the hall, leaving her plate with the half-eaten cream pie behind.

NINE

JENET RESISTED THE urge to sigh as he examined the dislocated shoulder of the soldier in the light of the lanterns crowding his desk. It was always broken arms and strained wrists with this lot. Young, overeager, all clamoring to prove their manhood by training too hard and pushing their bodies to the limit.

The window was open, letting in night air and the sound of crickets. If he closed his eyes, he could imagine himself back in his house in Tasglorn with the gardens a step away and the city spires glimmering on the horizon, not this little huddle of huts they called a town.

He was a nobleman's son, trained at the finest university in Sythra. He should be operating on senators, not attending to the shoulders of foot soldiers in the middle of the wilderness.

If he had only kept his eyes off that officer's daughter in Tasglorn, the one who smiled at him and whispered in the gardens how she loved him. If only he'd known her father was Cahan's second cousin. But no, he didn't, not before she was whisked away to be married at once, and he summoned for reassignment. Jenet was lucky he was only banished to the backwater country, and not the bottom tier of a Tasnian prison or a traitor's burial hole.

"This will hurt," he told the frightened soldier, barely more than a boy, who was sweating like a horse in labor. Jenet handed the lad a stick to bite and readied himself to pop the shoulder back into place.

This was his favorite part. Something about the way they yelled made him feel slightly better.

Someone banged on the door, calling his name. He released the soldier's arm and picked up his spectacles.

"What is it?"

The guard leaned against the doorframe, panting.

"What is it?" Jenet repeated, irritable.

"Sir," he said. "One of the prisoners..."

Jenet sighed at the word *prisoner*. The fort's dungeon was built for prisoners of war, but rarely did they have anyone to put in it besides the occasional young buck wanting to protest the actions of the soldiers by throwing eggs at the walls or shouting out curses on Prince Cahan.

"What about them?" he demanded.

The soldier licked his lips. "Sick as a pig."

Jenet swore under his breath. In a fort like this, with the barracks and the overcrowding... Sickness would spread like floodwaters.

He had to make sure it wasn't something to cause alarm.

"Wait here," he said to the soldier with the dislocated shoulder as he went to the door to join the guard.

"It's the young girl," the guard said as they walked. "They told me you treated her yesterday."

The girl at dinner. His irritation melted into concern. She'd shown signs of spotted fever, a dangerous, contagious disease if not treated properly at once, but he'd given her the herbs that he had to cut off the infection before it could spread enough to cause true concern. She'd taken them and thanked him, and he'd heard her sniffle a little as his back was turned. He imagined she hadn't had a great deal of sympathy as of late, and he supposed she was suffering from the effects of her ordeal. And of course the Seekers would insist upon keeping her in the dungeon and following cold procedure instead of acting like decent human beings. Or human beings at all, for that matter.

He followed the guard through the corridors of cold stone, down the spiraling staircases lit with torches, a scene that felt like something out of a children's fairytale. He despised this fort, a wasteful excess of space, always drafty, always damp, whether it was summer or winter. In his mind, he imagined what he might be doing in Tasglorn. Attending a dinner, perhaps, with live entertainment in the gardens and music that wafted over the lawns while the guests dined on roasted swan. A beautiful lady might be smiling at him over her glass, begging him for a story from the war front.

"Tell me about those dreadful Monarchists," she'd say. "Are they as murderous as the papers say?"

And everyone around them would lean in, wanting to hear, urging him to share a memory.

He would stretch back in his chair, murmuring *hmmm* as he took a sip of his wine and searched for the perfect story to tantalize them with—not too gory, but just thrilling enough to have his listeners entranced and horrified in equal measures. Granted, his stories were mostly about soldiers with sprained wrists from training, but in his imagination, he would tell about the time Monarchists stormed the fort and took him hostage at sword-point before he wrestled the blade away from the leader and severed the man's head from his shoulders in a single swipe.

The woman would gasp and press her handkerchief to her lips, delighted but pretending faintness for propriety's sake, and then he would modestly add that he'd received a medal of honor and a new post for his bravery in saving the commander and the rest of the fort, and that he was set to depart for Sythra within the week. Then everyone would congratulate him, their eyes wide as they repeated it. Sythra, where the fires burned from Monarchist rebels, where the soldiers marched into villages to subdue unruly crowds, where men were found hanging from bridges with their stomachs cut.

The moldy stench of the dungeons roused Jenet from his daydream as he stepped through the groaning door behind the soldier. The clammy air clung to his skin and made him feel moist, ill.

"Where is the girl?"

Perhaps after that, in this daydream of his, he would go on to tell of the time he tenderly nourished a sick girl, wrongfully accused of being a spy by Monarchist machinations, and how he drew her back from the brink of death in a cell beneath the fort. It would be the perfect contrast to his tale of bloodshed, this story of warmth and gentleness. He was, after all, a man of many facets. The listeners would sigh, happy to hear she'd recovered and gone on to a happy life in

Tasglorn, married to an officer in the army after Jenet healed her. Drawn from the brink of death, she was, he'd tell them. Had spotted fever...

They would all gasp. Spotted fever? They'd heard about how those in the throes of affliction bled from their eyes, their noses. He was a hero for daring to care for the girl at all. A saint.

The daydream kept him company as the guard led him down a narrow hall lined with metal bars. Most of the cells were empty except for a few scattered batches of straw and rags. Moonlight filtered through the slitted windows. The air smelled like something was rotting just out of sight.

Jenet yanked a handkerchief from his pocket and pressed it to his nose. It was difficult to imagine anything now, with such a stench.

"There," the guard said, pointing to the cells at the end of the row.

The girl lay curled in one of the individual cells, half-covered with straw. The dim light from the lanterns on the wall flickered over her body, making shadows where her hair fell over her eyes.

Jenet stepped forward and looked to the guard to open the door of the first cell. The man fumbled with the keys.

The cell door squealed on rusted hinges. Jenet stepped inside, his foot hitting an empty food bucket. A fly rose lazily from the interior and buzzed toward the window.

The prisoner lay on her side, bundled tight in the green dress she'd worn the day before at dinner, the rest of her heaped with straw as if in an effort to keep warm even though the room was sweltering from the leftover heat of the day. Hang these barbarous Seekers for keeping her in such squalor. Jenet crouched down beside her and reached out a hand to the silent shape of girl.

"Miss? Are you all right?"

A clump of her dark hair came off in his hand as her head lolled beneath his touch. Jenet recoiled in horror. Was she dead?

"Miss?" He bent over her with greater urgency, shaking her shoulder. "Miss Briand?"

This time, her head turned toward him, and he fell back in surprise. A guard, drugged and drooling, reeking with the sharp scent of what Jenet recognized as one of his sleep serums. He pulled away another clump of dark hair that had been bound to the guard's head to flop down and hide his face. The dress was tucked around him in shining folds. Underneath, the guard was trussed with ropes of rags.

Jenet took in the scene with a knot of dread in his stomach. They'd all been taken for fools. "Sound the alarm. Inform the Seekers. She's... she's escaped."

~

Auberon threw open the doors to the ramparts and strode out into the night. A thousand curses crowded on his tongue as he scanned the black waters of the lake.

She was gone, along with the traitor.

Men had already gone after them in the night, down the river in boats and along the sides on horseback. He knew they wouldn't find anything.

Lightning rent the sky in the distance, and the wind tossed his hair into his eyes. The storm that had been threatening all day was coming. The energy of it danced along his arms, lifting the hair. Calys stepped onto the rampart behind him, but he didn't turn.

He stared at the blackness and waited for her accusation.

"You read the traitor's mind. He was planning nothing. He was loyal." She paused, giving him a moment to speak. A moment to incriminate himself, admit he'd made a mistake or covered up a truth.

"Perhaps she overpowered him."

"That slip of a girl?"

Auberon reined in his anger with a flare of his nose. "What does it matter? I will find them in a matter of days. I will summon Hunters."

"Hunters?" Calys said. "Why so determined, if she was nothing, as you say?"

He swung around, letting his anger out for a moment, letting her believe it was due to him being indignant at the mere suggestion that he had lied. "What are you suggesting?"

Calys stayed silent but raised one eyebrow.

Auberon seethed, and then he laughed, because it was absurd and because it was the perfect cover for his true reasons. That's all she thought it was. "I am not *attracted* to her. I told you already."

Calys gave a small shrug. "It's a lonely place out here in the wilderness. No one would blame you if your tastes had grown a little eclectic."

Auberon shook his head. He turned back to the lake, formless in the dark, the sound of the water lapping far below making him restless.

He would find her.

TEN

BRIAND'S PADDLE CUT through the water as the land slipped by and thunder sounded in the distance behind them. Above, the night sky broiled with churning clouds, and rain fell in a steady drizzle. Her pulse drummed in her throat, and her mouth was dry with the thrill of escape, but the space between her shoulder blades itched as if waiting for an arrow.

Their clever rouse would be discovered before long, if it hadn't been already, and then the Seekers would give chase.

She was wearing the clothes Reela made for her again, and although she wanted to wash them free of their accumulated grime, she was glad to be out of that stifling dress with its itchy lace, slippery silk, and confining bodice. In her own clothes, she breathed freely. The energy of it made her paddle fast, her arms strong with the mixture of anger and fear that spurred her forward, away from her captors, toward uncertainty that might be freedom.

Kael said nothing as they glided over the water. He was maddeningly calm despite the danger at their heels.

Questions still simmered, unspoken, in Briand's mouth. Was she Kael's companion in escape or his prisoner once more? She wasn't sure what he thought, or what he would do when she tried to leave.

Finally, lights glimmered over the water through a mist of rain. A fishing village. Docks and piers straggled over the river, lanterns glowed from the houses. Rain hissed against the water. They drew the boat up at an empty dock and climbed out, the boat dipping and rocking behind them.

They needed supplies.

The trading post connected to an inn that hung over the edge of the river. The water slapped at the posts beneath their feet, sucking at the pilings as Kael and Briand stepped through the doorway of the inn and into a room thick with pipe smoke and laughter. Rain dripped from the ceiling with fat plops into buckets. Men and women crowded around tables, some holding cups of a thick, dark liquid that smelled strong enough to kill fish.

Kael steered her toward the trading post, just a countertop along one wall with shelves of goods behind it. Briand gripped her knife and scanned the crowded room as she followed him, half-expecting to see Auberon or Calys sitting in the corner, watching them and laughing at their stupidity. But there was no sign of the Seekers or their men.

The innkeeper bustled over to attend to them, wiping his hands on his apron. He asked no questions about why they were buying supplies in the middle of a stormy night instead of finding a bed to sleep in. He didn't even blink at them when Kael declined the offer of a room. Briand wondered how often people drifted through this village in the darkness, on the run from something or someone.

Kael produced a bag from a secret pocket and sorted out the coins in his palm. He purchased two bedrolls, a pair of canteens, two cloaks with thick, water-repelling otter fur for the outer layer, a pan for cooking, and an assortment of food.

The innkeeper set it in a pile on the counter and wiped his nose with his wrist as he asked, "Anything else?" in a gruff grunt of words.

Kael looked at Briand with a brow raised.

"That knife," she said, nodding at the mid-sized blade on the wall. Hers was simply too small for anything but the most delicate of uses.

Kael gave her a sideways glance that might have been reproving, but he laid down another coin anyway. After all, it had been her little knife that had helped them escape. She deserved it. "And the knife."

She felt foolish, like a child who'd asked for a sweet. She thought of her bag of coins that she'd amassed over the months in Gillspin, still buried in the thief-queen's den, and something inside twisted with longing. She tucked the newly-purchased knife away in the sheath sewn into her boot.

"Have you ever accidentally stabbed yourself?" Kael asked as they turned away from the counter. "You've got more metal on you than a pincushion."

Briand gave him a look to let him know that he insulted her by asking, and absolutely not. "Don't pretend you aren't armed to the teeth."

A boy brushed past them, head down, bumping into Kael with his shoulder. Kael's arm shot out and closed over the boy's wrist, pulling him back.

"Give it back," he said, calm and firm.

The boy squirmed. "I ain't got nothing," he protested, but Briand reached into the boy's pocket and pulled out Kael's coin bag. She shook it in his face.

"*Nothing* sounds a lot like my friend's coins. How strange."

The boy pulled away, and Kael let him go. He tucked his money bag back into his shirt. Briand watched where he put it, and he met her eyes with a measured smile. "Friend?"

"It's a figure of speech."

They found a table in the farthest corner of the inn to sort the things before leaving. The hum of voices and the pounding of the rain on the roof created a roar of noise that drowned out their voices as they spoke.

"We'll head down the river Jessu until we reach Lanternglorn," Kael said. "It should take two days, if the water stays high. He paused to check her expression, and she nodded agreement.

And after that? She wanted to ask. But she didn't, not yet. Not in this inn. She felt unsettled, off-kilter from the escape into damp darkness. She wanted to feel more in control when she demanded answers. She was still scrambling for footholds right now.

She busied herself with the things on the table.

They split the food into two packs and rolled it in the cloaks. Her stomach growled with hunger at the sight of the dried meats and cheeses. Kael must have noticed, for he ordered a round of hot drinks, not the dark liquid the fishermen were drinking, but something light that smelled like apples. Briand sniffed hers while Kael tipped his head back, drinking slowly, savoring. She tasted it, and the drink was like sunshine on her tongue.

"What is this?" she asked.

He finished his drink. "Naqa, from Estria. It's made from sunfruit. Gives the one who drinks it energy."

She took another sip and felt warmth spread through her veins.

Kael was watching the room even though he appeared focused on the cup he'd curled his fingers around. Briand could see the way he noted that the innkeeper had gone to the door to relight the lantern, the way he took stock of the others in the room and whether they carried weapons.

She frowned. It made her wonder what he observed about her.

"Do you think they'll be looking for us to be together?" she asked. "Is there any chance they will believe us to have parted ways?"

"Once they discover our escape, they'll know we worked together," Kael said.

Outside, the rain began to fall harder. A white mist formed over the docks. One of the questions forced itself from her lips before she could catch it. "Why did you help them capture me? When you heard they were looking for me, you could have arranged it so I escaped instead. You could have let me go."

She folded her arms, heart beating wildly, and waited for his answer. She tried to look uncaring. Her features felt clumsy and betraying. She swallowed around the dryness in her throat. You could have left me in my abandonment is what she didn't say. What she wanted to say, to see his reaction. But it was too honest. Too vulnerably raw.

Kael took his time with his answer. He seemed to be choosing the right words. "The Seekers aren't the only ones who want you back," he said finally.

She absorbed his meaning. Prisoner, or ally? Which was it? Had he let the Seekers capture her for him so he could procure her loyalty with his rescue? Or was it merely more convenient that way?

"Where are the others?" she asked instead.

Kael's eyes flicked to her and then away to the door. He set down the cup instead of answering. "Later. We should go."

The rain enfolded them as they left the inn, soaking their clothing and running down their faces in rivulets. Briand shaded her eyes from the water with one hand as they climbed back into the boat. The bottom sloshed water, and she used the bail-cup to throw it out as Kael untied the rope and pushed them away from the dock with his oar. The current caught them and dragged them out into the middle of the river.

Lanternglorn, Kael had said. They were headed for Lanternglorn.

The night was a blur of rain and darkness, punctuated by lightning. The river swelled, eliminating the need for rowing, and so for hours, they steered around rocks and trapped tree trunks that rose from the water. Her hands began to cramp from the wet and the cold and from gripping the oar. Then the river was roaring, and the rain falling so hard Briand couldn't see more than a few inches in front of her. Water puddled in her clothing and filled the bottom of the boat once more.

The boat pitched forward, propelled by a wall of water. A rock rose from the gloom ahead, too fast to steer around—CRACK—and she was flying from the boat.

She hit the water hard, a smack of icy chill and a mouthful of muddy river, and then she was swirling in a prison of bubbles and debris. She was swept down, or up, she couldn't tell. Her lungs were burning, burning, BURNING, and then she found the rock and clung to it, crawled up it, shoved herself upward out of the river and gulped air.

"Briand!" Kael's voice tore through the storm. She reached for him, blind with the rain, and their hands met. She pulled him from the river to the rock, and he clung to it around her.

ELEVEN

BRIAND WAS UP to her neck in dark water, her legs dangling in nothingness, her heart beating at a gallop as she gripped the edge of the rock. Kael breathed raggedly into her neck. She could feel his heartbeat against her shoulder blade, reminding her they were both still alive by some miracle.

"We've got to get to shore!" he shouted above the roar of the river, and then he had one arm around her tight and the other swung wide in the river as he kicked his legs with powerful strokes, propelling them toward land.

Her feet touched shore, and she stumbled to her knees on the pebbled stretch of solid earth. Kael dropped down beside her, breathing ragged and coughing up water.

The sky split with white light overhead, and thunder crackled like the growl of a dragon. Rain beat against their backs, and the swelling river dragged at their feet. She struggled up, arms shaking with the effort. Kael crawled up to his knees and then helped her stand. They weren't safe yet. In the shelter of the forest, Briand vomited river water and then sagged back against a mossy trunk. The rain ran off the leaves, spraying her with mist. Dawn had begun to show in milky white light through the gloom, illuminating the trees around them through a fog of rainfall.

They'd lost everything when the boat capsized. The food, the bedrolls, even their cloaks. She felt for her knife and found it still strapped to her ankle by some miracle.

"What now?" she said to Kael.

He shook the rain from his eyes. "We go on foot. There's another town farther down. We can buy more supplies there." He pulled out his money pouch, and a few coins rattled when he shook it. They were not completely destitute, at least not yet.

She nodded. There was no use in debating the point. They had no other options, and they couldn't stay here by the river, waiting for the Seekers to find them.

They headed into the forest.

~

Kael and Briand followed the Jessu river, staying far away from the shore to not be noticed should soldiers come down the river, but close enough to not get lost. As dawn brightened, the rain lessened enough that Briand could see farther than the next tree. The river roiled with floodwater, surging from its banks in a muddy brown torrent of water that curled around the trees and rushed over rocks, making white rapids and swirling whirlpools where forest had once been. The forest around them hung close and thick, lush with green moss that covered the rocks and tree trunks, and waving ferns that brushed her knees as she walked. Vines dangled from curly, reaching tree branches. The air was noticeably warmer than Gillspin, a true spring.

"It's so warm," Briand said.

"The coastal region near Tasglorn is hilly and temperate," Kael said. "But here in the interior, the Spirral Mountains trap the clouds and keep the land wet."

The trees kept off the worst of the rain, but sudden showers of icy water doused them whenever they pushed through a particularly dense thicket that had accumulated rainwater. Once, they startled an animal that went crashing through the thicket ahead. Briand was halfway up a tree before she realized it was only a deer.

They drank rain water from the leaves, letting it dribble into their mouths and down their chins. When the light was brighter, mid-morning, the rain began to lessen, and they journeyed more quickly through the thick vegetation. The sun reached its zenith, just a bright glowing spot behind the blanket of clouds barely visible through the forest top. Rain fell in misty spurts now, starting and stopping without warning. Briand picked a handful of berries, and the juice stained her fingers purple.

By the time the clouds began to grow purple-black with nightfall, she was stumbling in exhaustion.

"We should sleep," Kael said as he caught her for the third time.

They found a place in the underbrush to curl up out of sight.

Briand shut her eyes, and almost at once, she was dreaming that she was lying on a bed of straw in the cell again, with Auberon gazing at her through the bars. The sky outside was scudded with clouds that covered the stars. The cell was dim, Auberon just a dark shadow.

"You," he said. His voice was a blade sheathed in velvet. He curled his fingers around the bars and leaned closer. His eyes glinted. "You won't get away from me. I sent Hunters to track you."

"You'll never find me," she said, and then she pulled her knife from her hair and flung it at him.

She woke before she saw the blade hit, heart pounding, head aching. Kael crouched in the vegetation beside her, one hand on her shoulder and a finger to his lips. She heard voices and the stamp of feet.

Soldiers.

Kael lay beside her, his cheek pressed in the mud. They were nose to nose in the midst of the still-falling rain, his hair wet and splayed over his forehead and ears. His hand was an inch from hers. She listened to the sound of boots and kept her eyes trained on that hand. A snake wriggled over his knuckles, but he didn't flinch.

The boots passed inches from their heads.

When everything was still, he raised his head, shoulders and back taut as he pushed himself up enough to see.

"They're gone," he said, and she climbed to her feet. The rain began to fall harder again, mixing with the mud on their faces and washing it into streaks.

Her stomach rumbled, and she swayed. She'd eaten only berries since the previous night.

Kael studied her. "We are almost to the town I spoke of. Are you—?"

"I'm fine," Briand said.

He watched her, things unspoken in his eyes, before starting off again. She followed, willing her feet not to stumble this time, picking carefully around the mossy roots that thrust up from the ground, slick with rainwater and mud. The memory of the dream lingered in her bones like dread.

I sent Hunters to track you.

It was only a dream. She banished it from her thoughts and focused on following Kael through the gloom.

~

Lanternglorn was yet another river town, this one built around a brackish lagoon that formed where rocks bit off a piece of the river, diverting it into a shallow series of large pools. Vines drooped from the trees into the water, looking like hanging snakes in the darkening light. The town curled around the water's edge, boats pulled up to the docks, the whole thing up on stilts like tiptoes. The water surged at the top of the platforms and walkways, angry-brown and churning, a floodwater. Lights burned in the windows, and the tinny sound of laughter and music spilled into the rain-soaked air as they trudged toward the inn that was the centerpiece of the place, picking around the washed-out paths deep in water.

Kael paused to slosh river onto his cheeks, washing away the streaks of mud. He wiped his face with the edge of his cloak and wrung it out, droplets splattering at his boots. The money pouch jingled faintly, that click of coins the only thing between them and no dinner. He pulled it out and sorted the coins in his palm.

There weren't as many as she'd hoped.

"Come," Kael said, nodding once at the inn.

They stepped inside, pausing on the stoop as the water pooled around their feet. The whole floor was slick with mud, and nearly everyone inside had wet hair and damp clothing. But a fire burned in the fireplace on the wall, and drinks were flowing, and there could be no work with the river so high, so people crowded around tables, flushed and determinedly merry. Their laughter had an edge, and several men pulled away from their drinks to eye the pair of newcomers speculatively, as if Briand and Kael were cattle and the townsfolk were wondering what they might sell for.

Kael gathered calm around him like a cloak, and despite herself, Briand stepped a little closer to him. She put a hand on her knife, thankful to feel it beneath her fingers. They found a table, and Kael held up a finger for a serving maid, who bustled to them and returned with drinks and bowls of stew. Briand practically inhaled hers, ravenous. Kael ate slowly, watching the room.

"What is it?" Briand finished eating and wiped her mouth with her wrist. She knew him enough from his steward days to read that wrinkle between his eyebrows that smoothed away whenever anyone looked at him. He was concerned.

Kael shook his head, distracted.

She scanned the tables. No sign of Seekers.

"We should go soon," he murmured. He laid down coin for the food and crossed the room to buy supplies from the innkeeper. She wondered what he would get for the paltry sum left in his pouch. She sipped on her drink, which was just watery apple ale. It tasted like mud.

When he returned, Kael carried a bag that was disappointingly limp.

A young man whose arms looked like reeds inside his shirt and whose hair stuck up in a nest of curls stopped by their table with a basket of bread on his shoulder.

"Penny bread?" he asked, waggling the basket at them.

Briand's stomach clenched at the warm, honeyed scent. If only she had her Dubbok cards and a little time, she could generate her own income.

The young man squinted at her face. "You look familiar."

"Just traveling through," Kael remarked. His voice had an edge to it.

The young man glanced at Kael. "You look familiar too."

It was then that she noticed the paper pinned to the beam in the center of the room, a paper scrawled with two faces. Hers and Kael's.

Reward, the words beneath them read. *Dead or alive.*

She couldn't make out the amount, but it looked large.

"He recognizes us," Kael said as soon as the boy moved on.

"Did you see the sign?" She nodded toward the reward poster.

"Yes. But we have another problem. Someone's watching us."

She straightened, her spine stiffening.

Hunters?

"Don't look. Stand up, but do it slowly," he said. "Don't arouse any suspicions."

She set down her drink and rose. Kael shifted his cloak, and she saw him slip a knife into the sleeve of his shirt as he did so. He picked up the bag again and started toward the door when she saw them, in a corner at the end of the room.

Two men, dressed in drab colors, with eyes that were too sharp and faces that were too sober. Something about them was predatory. Elite. Not like the other sops in this backwater bar.

They rose as she walked past. A chill lanced her belly and spread to her legs. She forced herself to walk calmly. She trailed Kael out, and when they were in the open air again, she gulped a breath, her head buzzing with nerves.

"The men back in the tavern—?"

"Not who I'm worried about," Kael said. "Those are just the watchdogs. Come on."

They threaded through the houses toward the forest. The door of the inn opened and shut behind them, a rush of noise and light.

"This way," Kael muttered, moving quicker. The trees were visible beyond the buildings now.

They rounded a corner and ducked down an alley, boots splashing through puddles. A shadow appeared at the end of the alley, half obscured by the mist. Moving toward them.

The nape of Briand's neck prickled as a figure took shape. Tall. Hooded. Something about it felt wrong. Dead.

Another joined it.

"Run," Kael said.

She ran.

TWELVE

BRANCHES TORE AT Briand's hair and face as she plunged into the forest. The sky had darkened enough that she could see only a dim outline of trees around her. She slipped on the mud, falling, getting up again. Rain began falling again, thick and hard.

A soft sound like the scrape of a blade over silk hissed behind her, sending a jagged dart of alarm through her. She ran faster, tripping and clawing through the brush as Kael cried out once behind her, a muffled sound of pain, and she saw him stagger. She slipped as she tried to turn back. It was dark.

She scrambled up a tree, hands scraping the bark. Kael had vanished in the curtain of foggy rainfall. She heard the sound again, but this time, it was almost a whimper of metal. She pressed back against the tree.

Where was Kael?

She finally spotted him crouched against the trunk of a nearby oak, hand against his shoulder. His face was knit with pain. They must have hit him with something.

Briand waited until she almost couldn't stand it, and then she dropped from the tree. Her mind told her to run, but she ignored it.

She found Kael and helped him stand. He leaned heavily against her.

"We have to hide," she murmured in his ear.

"This way," he said, voice shot through with pain. "I know a place."

The rain slogged down, relentless, and they slipped into the cover of nightfall, heading south again.

~

Kael led her to a hollow place where two giant rocks rested together to form a cave. The ground was miraculously dry, and he found a pair of rocks and a few scrabbles of kindling at the back of the cave. Briand crouched in the shelter of the rock, watching as he whispered something into the kindling, striking the rock, and flames leaped forward, a little whiter and brighter than normal fire.

Briand tried to quell the emotion pumping through her as she watched him. She shook all over. The memory of him below in the forest, injured and trapped, made her throat close up with fear. Seeing him here before her, still breathing and frowning and making life difficult, gave her a strange and baffling sense of happiness. She knew she was an utter fool to feel this way, and yet she was powerless to stop it.

Kael sat down and pried his shirt away from his shoulder. A narrow cut seeped blood. It looked like a knife wound.

She must have been scowling, for Kael murmured, "I won't die and leave you here alone, Catfoot. It's just a small wound."

"What hit you?"

Kael winced as he flexed his arm. The flames flickered over his face, throwing shadows over his eyes. He was unexpectedly beautiful, she realized. She felt foolish and angry and embarrassed to even notice.

"I think it was a whisset," he said.

Briand squinted at him over the fire. "Explain," she said.

He stretched out one leg and then the other, as if testing for injuries. "Mechanical devices that stay strapped to the wrists of the user unless they are sent out to sting. They fly like arrows but return to their masters. Sometimes barbed, sometimes dipped in poison. Sometimes both. Used by bounty collectors, and sometimes Hunters."

Hunters. A shudder slid over her skin.

Kael studied her. "Do you know about the hierarchy?"

She'd learned bits and pieces in the last two years, listening whenever others whispered around the fireside, assembling a patchwork of knowledge about the people who wanted her dead thanks to the magic in her blood. "The Seekers have four divisions, I think."

He nodded. "Clerics are the lowliest. They handle small matters, mundane atrocities. They are usually petty, obsessed with what little power they have. Rule-followers, to the last. Healers, despite their name, mostly take people apart. They are scientists more than doctors, though they can mend bone and knit flesh. And you've met a Sighted. They are the ones most people think of when they think of Seekers. The gloved hands, the mind-reading, the torture."

Auberon.

Kael continued, "Sighted are the royalty in the hierarchy, the ones who give the orders and compose the councils. They can pluck thoughts from men. And the Hunters... they chase down enemies, defectors, and heretics."

"Were those Hunters who chased us?"

"Maybe."

She thought again of her dream and shivered. She looked away from him, at the mouth of the cave. The dark waited, black as old blood. They were hunted. They were almost without food, and they had no supplies. And now Kael was wounded.

Kael tore off a strip of the bit of his shirt that was least muddy. He was trying to bind his wound with his good hand and his teeth. Briand turned her head back to him, and after a moment, she scooted to his side and took over. He sat back, letting his breath whistle through his teeth as she tugged the bandage tight. She could feel him studying her as she worked. She tied the excess in a knot and drew back.

The air thickened with unspoken things once more.

"What if you've been poisoned?" she asked.

"We'll meet up with a Monarchist I know who can give us shelter," Kael said. "He'll protect us both while I heal."

"I'm not part of your schemes anymore," Briand said. "I only want to get away."

There. She'd said it baldly now, and he would probably answer, and she would know what she was to him now. But as she spoke the last part, she felt a tug in her chest telling her it was not quite true. Escape wasn't the only thing she wanted.

Did she want him to disagree with her protest? To insist she was his prisoner? Or did she want him to let her go without a fight? She didn't even know the answer. She was angry suddenly, and the anger obscured the finer points of feeling.

The curve of Kael's face was half-obscured in the darkness, but she could tell he was angry too. "You can't run away from duty this time, Briand. You are as much a part of this as I."

Duty. The word was a slap in the face. She laughed roughly, her anger fanning hot, and she let it grow to drown out the useless other feelings inside her. "I have no duty to your Monarchists."

She wanted to pick a fight. She wanted him to be angry with her. It was better than sitting here with him so coldly composed while she burned with this unwelcome emotion. This... this attraction.

"The reason runs in your veins," he said. "You stole the vial and drank it. *You* chained yourself to this."

And she was continuing to chain herself, hopelessly, with every feeling she harbored for him and the others. And she was angrier still, this time at herself.

"They will come for you no matter where you go. Everyone will be looking. There's a reward for us now. You saw the paper."

"No," she whispered fiercely. "The Seeker said I wasn't a dragonsayer. I can go wherever I like now, and they won't follow. I can change my appearance, my name—"

"But he lied," Kael said. "The Seeker lied. He knows who you are."

"He couldn't read my mind," she said. "As far as he knows, it is true."

Kael went still. "What did you say?"

Briand paused, inwardly cursing her stupidity. She hadn't intended to tell him, at least not yet. But Kael had ignited fury and fire in her, and she'd forgotten to hold her words closely.

She repeated it reluctantly. "He couldn't read my mind. He visited me earlier and tried again. He doesn't know what I am."

Kael stared at her a moment, absorbing this. "Well, that will be useful."

"I'm not a Monarchist," she repeated.

"No, you made that much clear when you abandoned your post and fled to Gillspin to live among thieves and beggars."

"Thieves and beggars who didn't abandon me," she said, although it wasn't exactly true.

His eyes blazed. He didn't defend himself. "And the Hermit? When did he abandon you?"

Briand clammed up at the mention of the Hermit, her lips white as she pressed them together.

He would want her gone if he knew the truth of what had happened that night.

Kael leaned his head back against the stones. His sigh was laced with pain. "We're going to need to work together to survive this. I can't let you go, Catfoot. Not yet. They're going to keep coming for you. And we need you."

She wanted to laugh, a derisive *ha*, but the sound stuck in her throat. "Then perhaps you should try to bribe me."

"What do you want, Briand?"

He'd surprised her. She took a moment to answer. "My father's house," she said. "I want my father's house." Just speaking the words filled her with a heavy, aching hope. Maybe if she could get back to that place, she could find her moorings again.

Kael turned his head.

"What is it?" she asked.

Silence blanketed them as Kael chose his words. "Your father's castle was burned to the ground last winter in a riot, a protest against Cahan. So they say."

For a moment, Briand couldn't breathe.

"Does Bran know?" she managed. Just saying his name made her eyes sting.

Kael nodded, sober. "He was there."

She pictured it, ashes floating like dust motes in the air, pale as snow as they drifted down amid blackened ruins of the walls. Bran, standing in the center of a pile of ash, embers at his feet. Her lungs were too tight as she saw it in her mind's eye, her head throbbed. She leaned back against the stone and tried to swallow the rush of burning bile that filled her throat.

"You should sleep," Kael said finally.

Weariness stretched over her, heavy and smothering. She didn't want to shut her eyes, the dark was waiting, but exhaustion claimed her.

~

The words *burned to the ground* still rang in her ears when she woke in the middle of the night and found Kael pale and sweating, feverish, his jaw locked with pain.

Poison, she thought, and fear fluttered in her belly.

The fire was low, and she stirred it with a stick and added fuel, making the flames dance again. They were plain flames now, with no magic in them. Kael watched her build up the fire. He took a swallow of water from the canteen among their provisions and leaned back against the stones. His lips were white.

"This would be the perfect time to run," Briand said without looking up.

"And yet you haven't," Kael replied. His voice was low, thick with pain, husky, but he kept his head up, his eyes trained on her firmly. As if he was still as capable as always.

"You think you know everything about me," Briand said, angry now. The anger was always within easy reach, leaping up as easily as the fire when stoked. Anger was her shield. "You don't."

Kael's mouth flexed, a thin and painful smile. "I haven't the slightest idea what goes through that head of yours half the time. But you get a look like you're a cat about to pounce, and I know it will be trouble, whatever it is."

She could leave, she thought, eyeing the doorway. She could stand up and walk away now, before the light came back.

No, she was lying to herself.

There were still words to be said, and things to be known, and the silence between them was like a chain on her heart.

Instead, she poked at the fire until it blazed hot and Kael's breathing slipped into an even, soft rhythm.

~

In the morning, they ate a portion of the food cold and set off again. Kael's face was knit with pain, but he could stand on his own. Still, she worried.

The rain had lifted and the clouds scattered, leaving the forest dripping but flush with sunlight. Deer fled before them, crashing in the underbrush. A flutter of birds startled up from the narrow path, a flash of white and gold-striped feathers.

Briand walked ahead, pushing branches out of the way, warring with herself. The words she and Kael had exchanged the night before still echoed in her mind, taunting her, pulling at her. Each word was like a hook in her flesh.

The forest began to grow thicker, lusher. The trees became massive, twisted things, blanketed in moss and vines. Purple flowers the size of Briand's fist drooped down in clusters, smelling like sugar. Tiny birds with wings in a blur darted among them, hovering for the blink of an eye and then flying away.

Kael moved tiredly. The bandage on his arm was stained dark, and he winced when he moved it. He didn't speak, reserving his strength for walking.

Briand flicked her gaze over him. Would he be able to walk for much longer?

"We should rest," she said, and Kael gave her a sharp look, but he dropped to a mossy rock anyway. She busied herself with the provisions, collecting water from a few leaves the size of platters. They'd strayed from the river, and she had lost her sense of direction and time. The forest was wrapped in a hush that made her feel small and sleepy. She needed to stay vigilant.

"Where is this Monarchist friend we're seeking?"

Kael's gaze was wary. "Why?"

"So I can find him to deliver your body if you go unconscious," she snapped.

At first she thought he wouldn't tell her, but then he said, "We're in the Verd now. It's the forest that runs along the center of the kingdom parallel with the mountains. We aren't too far from the camp. A few more hours, perhaps."

"Then we should be off," she said. "I don't know that you'll last more than a few hours."

He gave her a look that might have been challenging, but she was already turning to continue. Her heart wasn't into it to spar with him, not today, not when he looked half dead and worry gnawed at her ribs. Kael fell into step behind her, and silence swept over them, punctuated only by the sound of birds in the distance that quelled as they passed.

They stopped often to rest and eat a little of the dwindling food supply. Briand measured out the last portion as the sun was setting. Barely a mouthful for each of them. She swallowed a gulp of water and stood, brushing crumbs from her legs. Kael was stumbling under the weight of his bag. She took it from him and shouldered it without a word, and this time, he let her without arguing.

They'd found a path, a twisted, rocky strip of earth worn down by the passage of animals, and followed it until they met a clearing strewn with yellow leaves over the thick moss. It looked like a ballroom carpeted with tapestries after a great celebration. Sunlight slanted down in a glowing golden finger.

Briand stepped onto the moss and felt it sink beneath her feet like a thick woolen rug. She stopped to look around, and then took another step.

Kael shouted, his fingers grabbed her wrist, and they both tumbled forward as the ground opened beneath them into a black pit.

THIRTEEN

BRIAND LAY STUNNED, her cheek pressed against damp earth. Her knees burned, and one leg of her trousers was torn. The air was knocked from her lungs, and she coughed as it rushed back. Beside her, Kael struggled up. A scrape on his forehead dripped blood. He reached for her.

"Are you—?"

"I'm all right," she managed. "Only winded."

He took her face in his hands and turned it from side to side. She reached out and wiped the blood from his eyebrow. He smiled with half his mouth. His hand was still on her chin.

She was dizzy from the fall or his smile, she didn't know which. When he removed his hand, she felt colder.

Briand gazed up at the hole they'd fallen through. A circle of sky and leaves was visible, the light purplish. Dusk. She crawled forward and then climbed to her feet, looking around. The hole appeared to have been dug by hand. She sank her fingers into the dirt, and it crumbled away.

"Seekers?" she asked in a panic. "Hunters?"

Kael gave a shake of his head. "Monarchists. A band of them leads a small resistance in this part of Tasna."

"We've found them? Your friend?"

Kael hesitated, one brow drawing down as he grimaced slightly. "Friend might be too strong a word."

"What do you mean?" Alarm rose in her.

Kael gingerly pressed his hand along his head. He drew back his fingers, and they were red with a smear of blood. "We had... an altercation."

"Stop talking like Nath and tell me plainly. What kind of situation are we in, Kael?"

Footsteps sounded above them. A shadow covered the light as a face leaned over the pit.

"What have we caught in our trap?" someone called out in a sing-song tone. "Something we can skin for supper? Feed to the dogs?"

Kael straightened, his hand pulling away from hers. "Boot?" he called.

There was a pause.

"Who's asking?"

Kael closed his eyes for half a second. Tension sharpened his cheekbones.

"It's Kael," he called.

There was another silence from above.

"We've got three bows trained on you," a voice called down. "Take the ropes as they're lowered and we'll pull you up."

Briand and Kael exchanged a glance. Kael's forehead was dotted with perspiration. He said something, but Briand couldn't hear him. She looked up.

The ropes fell. Kael knotted one around his chest and nodded to her. Briand did the same and took hold of the rope with her hands and pulled to signal that she was ready. She braced one foot against the wall of earth as she began to rise, dragging against the side, dirt raining into her eyes. Below, Kael groaned as the rope put pressure on his injured shoulder.

Briand kept a hand on her knife. Her stomach jumped as she heard voices muttering above.

She reached the top and hands grabbed her. They hauled her up, and she was looking into the bearded face of a man with skin the color of walnuts and an uneven smile with broken teeth. Was this Boot?

He set her down a few feet from the hole and reached for Kael. Three other figures—two men and a woman—held crossbows, which they pointed at the hole. They were all dressed in green cloaks, with plain buckskin clothing beneath. Their faces were smeared with streaks of dirt, and they were thin, haggard, with hair that looked as though it had been hacked off with a knife.

The man dragged Kael from the pit. He was unconscious now.

"He's injured," Briand said as they laid him down on the moss. "Poison, I think. Can you help him?" She found to keep panic from her voice.

"Hmm." Boot crouched down and examined the bandage on Kael's shoulder. "What caused the wound?"

"A whisset."

At the mention of a whisset, the others exchanged a look among themselves, faces blanching.

"Are you still being pursued?" Boot asked, peering up at her and then at the forest beyond. He seemed wary, cold.

"Not anymore."

Kael's eyes flicked back open.

Briand swallowed her gasp of relief. She clenched her hands and stayed where she was as Kael drew himself up on his elbows.

The others still hadn't lowered their crossbows. Anger flared in Briand, and she wanted to snap at them to lower the blasted weapons, but she swallowed the emotions and kept her eyes trained on Kael and Boot.

"You've lost your mind for daring to come here," Boot said. He spoke quietly, as if for Kael's ears alone, but everyone could hear his words in the stillness of the clearing. "Ben wants retribution."

Kael coughed. The blood on his face was drying in a sticky-dark river that streaked from his eyebrow and temple down to his chin. "We had little choice."

"Or perhaps you have a trick up your sleeve. I've heard the rumors. They say you're a traitor to the cause."

Kael held Boot's gaze. "You know me better than that."

"I thought I did," Boot said. He stood. "What about her?" he said with a nod at Briand, still speaking to Kael. "Is she a spy, too?"

"She was a captive of the Seekers," he said. "We escaped together."

Boot murmured something under his breath at the word *captive*. He jerked his head at the others. "We don't have time to debate this here. This is unprotected ground, and these woods are filled with enemy soldiers on patrol. Carry him. We'll take them back with us to safer territory." He trained his gaze on Briand, then Kael again. "Surrender your weapons first."

Kael produced his blade, and Boot snatched it from him and tucked it into his belt. "And your shirt. Just to make sure you aren't hiding anything else."

Kael pulled off his shirt, moving slowly. His naked chest gleamed with sweat as he pulled the cloth over his head and tossed it at Boot with a wince at the movement. Scars made a pattern of pain down his sides.

Briand bit her lip. This charade of stripping to prove innocence was ridiculous.

"And the girl?" Boot said.

Anger burned at the back of her throat. "You want me to strip too?"

"Just your weapons," he said, amused.

"I thought we were allies." she said instead of surrendering her knife. "So far, I'm not impressed with this Monarchist's hospitality."

"We're hospitable to those we trust," Boot said.

"Ha," she retorted. "Seems we are at an impasse."

"Briand." Kael's head sagged to the side, and his eyes half closed.

After a moment's hesitation, she pulled out the knife sticking from her wrist sheath and handed it over, biting back words. She left the smaller one hidden.

"Blindfold and bind them. Both of them."

The woman produced two strips of cloth from her belt.

Briand bristled, but Kael reached out his arms in response, wrists together, holding Boot's eyes steadily as he did so. He was calm, infuriatingly so. When the woman tied the blindfold around his eyes, he looked as though he were going to his own execution.

Briand felt a rush of fear.

"You won't bind me," she said when they came to her. "I'm not surrendering. I've done nothing but ask sanctuary from our enemy."

Boot scowled.

"I'm the one you're afraid of," Kael said. "Let her be."

The crackle of brush signaled someone's approach. Everyone tensed, and then a thin, sinewy man with a thick scar down one side of his face and a patch over the opposite eye thrust himself through the branches and into the clearly. He froze at the sight of them.

"Kael," he said.

Kael's head jerked up. His eyes were hidden by the blindfold, but his mouth tugged down in a wry frown. "Ben."

An ugly tension hung over the scene. The hair on Briand's arms prickled, and her lungs couldn't seem to get enough breath in them. Boot said something to Ben, a whisper of words, a motion toward Briand. Ben replied in his ear, and Boot drew back.

Ben pulled out a knife.

Briand was between Kael and the knife before she had time to think about what she was doing. Her legs propelled her by pure instinct, and then she was staring down the knife.

"Step aside," Ben said.

"No!"

"Boot says you're harmless, and I've got no quarrel with you, but I'll kill you too if you don't move."

"You would stab an unarmed man with his hands still bound?" Her heart beat a staccato chant in her head. Her legs were stone and her stomach a storm.

"Absolutely. Kael is a master fighter. I'm taking no chances." He jerked his head at Boot, who stepped forward to drag her away. Ben lifted his arm, the knife arcing with a flash toward Kael.

"Kael!" Briand shouted.

Kael moved in a blur, grabbing Ben by his arm with both hands—still bound together—and flipping him to the ground. He turned, his blindfold halfway dislodged, knocking a second man who jumped to fight him on his back with a well-aimed kick. Briand broke away from Boot. She yanked her hidden knife from her hair and sliced at the woman who tried to apprehend her. She drew blood.

Briand stepped back until her shoulders bumped Kael's and they stood back-to-back. Briand's heart beat a wild rhythm against ribs and skin. She could feel Kael trembling from the exertion. She didn't know how he was still standing.

"Ben," Kael said, panting.

"Stop this," Briand said. She looked at Boot and then at Ben. "Why are you doing this? You're Monarchists just like him." Anger rose in her. She felt herself expanding, as if she were sending waves of power into the forest. A snake dropped from the trees and slithered toward them.

"This man is a traitor," Ben said, pointing his finger at Kael. "He deserves to be put down like a dog."

"With no trial? I'm sure your prince would have something to say about that. Is this the way of the Monarchists? Savage killing of your own in the forest thanks to a rumor?"

Ben paused. Her words had hit their mark.

"Ben," Kael said. "I serve the true prince. I always have."

The knife wavered in Ben's hand, and pressure mounted in Briand's head as fury blazed through her. Another snake slithered through the grass. A crack came from the forest to her right, the sound of a branch snapping like a bone.

Someone shouted. A roar cut through the sound, and a sick wet crunch, and then everyone was scattering, disappearing into the underbrush like rabbits as a blur of brown fur and long teeth knocked one of the Monarchists to the ground. Blood sprayed Briand as she staggered back.

The beast lifted its head from the fallen man, focusing yellow eyes on Ben. It was larger than a wolf, lizard-like, with a leathery plate-like back, curving teeth and a blunt, bloodied snout. It lunged, catching Ben's leg with its jaws.

Ben stumbled backward and fell to the ground beneath the beast. A few of the Monarchists fired at the creature from the trees, but the arrows bounced off its back. It hissed and spat, turning its head. Her mind spun, she was falling in and out of the creature's mind. It shook its head, snarling.

"Briand," Kael shouted at her. "Stop it!"

She tried, but it was slippery, and she couldn't get any kind of hold. This wasn't a dragon. It was barely a lizard-creature.

Then Kael was atop it, his still-bound hands around the creature's neck, squeezing hard. The beast thrashed, making a gurgling sound. Ben scrambled away as Kael continued to strangle the animal.

Its head began to droop beneath the pressure. Its legs thrashed, and it snapped its jaws, but the movements slowed, and finally stopped.

Kael rolled off the beast onto the ground and fainted.

Ben looked at the knife in his hand, and then at Kael. He took a step toward the man as the others rushed in.

"Dead," Boot reported of the creature.

"What is it?" Briand said, her pulse slamming furiously through her, her legs shaking. She caught a tree for balance.

"A casser monster," Ben said. "They're reclusive, usually. Sign of bad luck." He shook his head and looked down at his knife. His face hardened.

"He saved your life," Briand said.

"He's a traitor." But he sounded uncertain.

"The thief-queen's lot had more loyalty than you Monarchists," she said, disgusted. "He just *saved your life*. He needs care and rest so he doesn't die. Take care of your friend now. Debate the finer points of loyalty and treason later."

Ben stared at her a moment. Then, he reached past her with the knife, but only to slit the ropes that encircled Kael's wrists.

115

FOURTEEN

THEY REACHED THE Monarchist hideout after an hour of climbing into the hills. It was chiseled into the stone of the cave, with walls of stone arching up to a ceiling of dangling rock that looked like icicles. Narrow doorways opened into rooms for sleeping and bathing, separate from the main area where the fires burned, the flames too-bright and strange, a smokeless, magic fire like the one Kael had built.

By Ben's orders, men carried Kael away to the hideout's resident physician, leaving Briand standing alone until a woman directed her to a fireside, where she was given stew and bread. She sat on a rock beneath a hole in the cave ceiling open to the forest and sky above, eating fast, scanning the crowd. Kael's absence made her feel as though she were missing one of her knives. She looked for where they had taken him, wanting a reason to see if he was really being tended to, to see if he was not locked in a dungeon instead. But that seemed like a foolish idea at the moment. She should be thinking of a way to escape. But all she wanted was rest and food and assurance that Kael was going to live.

Still, she took note of the ways to exit the cave and ran through a few scenarios of escape in her mind while she ate. Such exercises steadied her hands as well as her emotions.

Ben dropped beside her on the rock with his own bowl of stew in his hands.

"Any word about Kael?" she asked.

"The doctor says he'll live. That's all I know." He paused. "You'll have to surrender your knife."

"Not happening," she said. "I'm not your enemy, but you're treating me like one."

He grunted. "You fought me a mere hour ago."

"I defended my life."

He scratched beneath his eye patch, and she caught a glimpse of a puckered scar where his eye would have been. "I am sorry you've witnesses the uglier side to our fight, girl," he said. "But traitors must be dealt with ruthlessly and immediately."

"I know about traitors," she said. She saw Drune's weathered face in her mind's eye, and she brushed a hand briskly across her lap, clearing away the crumbs of her meal. "I was delivered to the Seekers' hands for money."

Ben made a soft sound of disgust. "What happened to your betrayer?"

"They slit his throat."

He shoveled a bite of stew into his mouth. "Exactly what he deserved."

~

A woman with ice-white hair and a face marked with three scars directed Briand to one of the bathing rooms for a bath. Everyone among the Monarchists seemed to have scars.

She set a pile of clean clothing on a stone and handed Briand a bar of soap that smelled like lavender. A spring bubbled up from a hole in the ground, steam billowing into the air. After the woman left, closing a curtain behind her, Briand undressed from her mud-stiffened clothes and dipped into the water with a groan.

The water bubbled around her shoulders and crept up to the crown of her head as she sank down. She closed her eyes, relishing for a second the sensation of being clean and enveloped in warmth. She scrubbed herself with the soap, taking care to wash the mud from her hair and from every inch of her skin. When she'd finished, she floated in the water until her fingers and toes began to shrivel. Then she climbed from the bath, dried herself, and dressed in the clothes the woman had given her. They were similar to her own garments—plain brown trousers, a flowing shirt, and a leather corset that did not pinch or squeeze.

She dressed and then went to find Kael.

He lay on a mattress in one of the private sleeping rooms, a damp cloth draped across his forehead, and a fresh white bandage swathing his injured shoulder. He appeared to have been bathed, for his shirt had been removed, and his skin was clean of mud. The physician sat beside him, holding a vial of brown liquid.

Briand's chest seized at the sight of the vial. It reminded her of previous things.

"Catfoot," Kael said without opening his eyes.

She remained in the doorway as Kael drank the vial, a quick swallow, and then the doctor brushed past her, leaving them alone.

"How'd you know it was me?"

"You were playing with your knife. It makes a clicking sound when you tap your thumbnail against it."

She looked down at the blade, which had found its way into her palm during the walk. She slid the knife into its sheath without comment. By the flicker of firelight, his chest gleamed, and she saw a ripple of scars across his arms and shoulders. White lines that traced an untold story.

Kael turned in the bed toward her, finally opening his eyes. His gaze caught hers and held. She felt caught. Foolish. Transparent.

"Did I summon that creature that attacked Ben?"

Kael took a moment to respond. "That seems to happen with you and certain creatures."

Like the snakes. She nodded. She blinked away the images of him killing it.

"Ben says you'll live."

"Disappointed?" He said it lightly, a joke, but his mouth turned down at one corner. He moved in the bed, pulling up one knee beneath the sheet.

A knot of something hot and insistent built inside her. Perhaps it was the rush of shaky energy that came after the fight in the woods. Or was it the way Kael looked in that bed, naked beneath the bandages and scars, with his freshly washed hair against his neck and forehead? She felt as though she were betraying herself by not averting her eyes.

She was at war with herself. She felt herself drawn forward to the bedside, step by reluctant step. When she answered, she spoke roughly to hide the uncertainty and flush of awareness she had whenever he was near.

"I have no loyalty to your prince," she said. "Your Monarchist plans are nothing to me. I don't care who rules Austrisia. It all looks the same from the bottom of the barrel of society. I only want to live, and I'll do what I can to make that happen."

He took a breath. "Why are you so furious with me?"

The question was a punch to the gut. Thoughts and questions swirled in her mind. She wanted to accuse him. She wanted to defend him.

Kael pushed himself up with both arms and leaned back against the wall. The sheet was a splash of pale white against his brown skin. His hair brushed his eyes.

"You promised," she said, the words tasting like acid. "You promised, and you didn't come."

There it was, naked before them both. The admission made her feel raw. She felt foolish. Stupid. Insisting on promises in this world of guts and war. And yet—nothing had ever mattered to her more.

She wanted him to deny it so she could call him a liar again and watch his face tighten at the accusation, the way a man of honor does when he realizes his honor is nothing but dung. She wanted him to make excuses and see those excuses melt before him, pitiful in the face of what he'd done.

"I did come," Kael said.

Her mouth fell open. That was the last thing she'd expected him to say. "What?"

Kael's expression was as opaque as stone. "I came, and you weren't there."

Questions crowded her mind, memories of the night she'd left. When had he come? What had he found?

Before she could compose her reply, the doctor entered the room. "Out," he said gruffly to her. "He needs rest."

Briand slipped away, the questions unanswered.

~

Briand threw the knife again and again at her target, a stuffed mannequin leaking straw. Her blade kept hitting the very edge, like a needle slipping into a hem.

"Another inch and you'll miss the target entirely, my dear." Boot remarked behind her.

She walked to the target to retrieve the knife, ignoring his comment. "Why are you called Boot?"

"Because I'm told I have a face like one."

She laughed and threw her knife at the target again. This time, it missed the target entirely and sank into a tapestry on the wall, the blade buried in the neck of a horse depicted in vivid black.

"Need lessons?" he asked. "I could teach you."

She threw him a glance that stopped him from coming closer. "No. And I thought you wanted to take my knife."

"I did... but you don't appear to be much danger to us."

She ran a finger across the top of the knife. His patronizing was boring. "What do you want?"

"Briand, is it?" he asked.

She made a noncommittal sound. Had he been sent to get information out of her? Or was he here to flirt?

"I'm not a prisoner, then?"

"You are our guest," he said.

"You have a funny way of showing it." She threw the knife. A few flecks of straw fell to the floor as the blade hit the edge of the mannequin again.

"You've been given a bath, food, and clothing. Kael has been tended to by our physician."

"Yes, after you tried to kill us." She crossed the room to retrieve the blade and returned to his side. "You Monarchists all seem to think a few winsome words about duty and a little begrudging life-saving will fix everything."

He laughed. "It does, usually. We're a dutiful, loyal lot."

But not loyal enough to look for their missing guttersnipes. She turned the knife over in her hand, looking at it.

"I have some information about the Seekers your leader might find interesting," she said. Might as well get straight to it. This was what they wanted. She could smell the hunger for it on them. They were holed up in the mountains here. Ben had that air of a man who wants to be more important to his cause than he is. Information on the enemy might make him feel as though he had something useful to offer his prince. The desire to get it would make him malleable.

Boot straightened.

"But I have a few conditions." She retrieved the knife from the tapestry, pausing to finger the slit she'd made.

"Such as?"

"When we leave, Ben will give us, as befits guests, provisions for our journey. Food, clothing, weapons, bedding. Horses."

"Horses?" He laughed. "You ask for too much."

"I have information regarding what the Seekers are looking for, and what they want to do with it when they find it."

Boots appeared skeptical. She fixed her gaze on him.

"Have you heard of the dragonsayer?"

His eyes narrowed in a way that told her he had. She had him in the palm of her hand.

"Come and eat," he said. "And tell Ben what you know."

FIFTEEN

BRIAND SHEATHED HER knife and followed Boot into the large room, where pots bubbled over cook fires and a few brush hens turned on spits, the fat dripping into the fire and sizzling in the ashes. Men and women gathered around them, perched on benches and rocks to eat with their hands. Ben sat among them, eating, his shoulder bowed as if under great pressure.

Boot spoke in Ben's ear, then fetched Briand a bowl of food and sat beside her on the sandy floor. He ate ravenously, as did Briand. She had learned not to turn up her nose at a meal, and the meat had a savory, smoky flavor that reminded her of when she was a child and eating the venison the hunters brought back to the castle.

Ben approached a few moments later. He wore a look of grim determination as he settled beside her. Boot excused himself and went to the fire. Briand took a bite of stew as she waited for his question. Did they eat anything else here?

"Tell me about the Seekers," Ben said.

She swallowed before answering. "Send us away with provisions and supplies."

He paused, turning his head to look toward the fire. "I will do as you asked."

"Let them hear you say it." She nodded at the others.

"I will give you provisions for your journey. Food..." He paused. "And horses. I hope you appreciate the generosity."

"We're very grateful," Briand snapped.

He held out his hand. Briand looked at his palm and outstretched fingers, marred with scars, and then his face. She lifted an eyebrow.

"Your knife," Ben said. "For the oath."

The others watched their exchange. She handed her blade over reluctantly under the weight of those stares. He pressed the tip into his skin, and a bead of red gathered, quivering, in the middle of his palm. He turned his hand over, and the drop fell into the sand. He spit on it.

"It will be done," he said. "Now, talk."

"The Seekers are looking for the dragonsayer," she said.

Ben's brow furrowed. "I've heard only rumors, the stuff of fairy tales. You say the dragonsayer is real?"

"The Seekers think so," she said.

"What do the Seekers want with him?"

"They want to capture and take the dragonsayer to Tasglorn," she said.

"And they haven't found this dragonsayer?"

"They were still looking when we escaped," she said.

His mouth curved in a grim smile. "I've heard tales that he destroyed a bridge up north and called up dragons to eat the Seekers chasing him. No wonder they're afraid. Anything else?"

"The garrison where I was imprisoned was swarming with soldiers. Completely overflowing. I think they were preparing for something."

"What garrison?" Ben was extra alert. "We've had reports of extra movement to the north, between the Blue Mountains and along the river. Troops, supplies. They're preparing for something."

"We were in Carru when we escaped," she said.

"Carru," he repeated, frowning. "Interesting."

She told him a little more about what she'd observed, how the troops drilled with rifles. He nodded, asking occasional questions for clarity, until finally she fell silent.

"How exactly did you escape from a Seeker?" Ben leaned forward, propping his chin in his hand. A few of the others shifted a little closer, pretending to fuss with shoes or the fire. They were listening, too.

Briand licked her lower lip. It was a good story, so she raised her voice to let the others hear it properly. "I pretended to be sick," she said, smiling a little at the memory. "I was locked in the dungeon. One of the Seekers had taken a bit of an interest in me, and after some coaxing, he agreed to let me have a bath and eat dinner with the fort commander and officers."

People turned to listen.

"Naturally," she continued, "that required a fancy dress."

"What kind of dress?" a thin, dark-haired woman asked eagerly, as if she needed every detail to imagine it.

"Green," Briand said. "With embroidered flowers on the sleeves and neck." She brushed her fingertips across her shoulders and collarbone to illustrate.

"I bathed and put on the dress, but what they didn't know is that I had a knife stashed away, one they hadn't found when they'd captured and searched me."

Her listeners grinned and nodded.

"After I'd bathed, so my skin was clean and fresh, I used the dull edge of my knife against my skin, and I pinched and rubbed it just so..." She demonstrated, pantomiming. "And made blood blisters."

She paused. Did they understand?

"Spotted fever," Boot called out. "Clever."

The others murmured and chuckled.

"When I was dining with the commander, my wrist happened to find itself under the nose of his physician, who was alarmed to see the marks of a contagious and deadly disease on me."

Giggles ran through the crowd.

"He hurried me away to his room, where I snatched a bottle of sleeping salts when his back was turned."

They were all grinning.

"I slipped it into my bodice, and on the way back to my cell, I slipped a little in the guard's bucket of drinking water. After he'd succumbed to sleep, Kael was there to steal his keys and help me out of my cell. Of course, I couldn't have them discovering an empty cell when they came to look in on me, so I wrapped the slumbering fellow in my gown and covered his face with some of my chopped-off hair."

The Monarchists hooted and clapped. Boot whistled. Briand warmed with pleasure, reliving the moment, tasting the success once more. She felt a little giddy.

"Kael procured the boat," she said. "And we headed down the river. The storms capsized us, though, and we lost our provisions. When we stopped in a town to find more, we were chased by men with a whisset. Kael was injured, and we managed to hide and then make our way here."

She paused, flushed with the telling. They were watching her, an audience of admirers, and she breathed in the feeling of being looked at with such comradery. A feeling of longing fluttered in her chest, like a bird wrapped up tight and struggling to free itself.

"I bet the Seekers were fit to be tied," one woman cackled, and the rest of them laughed, a sound that seemed grateful to be freed from their throats, as if they didn't get to laugh often and almost forgot how.

"They sent Hunters after us."

Everyone turned to see him standing at the edge of the fire, his face gleaming in the flicker of orange flames, exhaustion written under his eyes. He'd put his shirt back on, hiding his scarred back once more.

Briand's smile faded. The others fell silent as the jovial mood cooled into uncertainty. The others gazed at him. They seemed to be torn between the account of him being a hero that they'd just heard, and their leader's feelings.

Ben stood, and the two men faced each other for an aching length of time.

"You killed the casser monster," Ben said finally. "You could have let it eat me."

"I could have," Kael agreed. "But I don't want you dead, Ben."

A few of those watching murmured. Ben looked wary.

"You're my friend," Kael said. "I haven't forgotten the Red Fields and the battle there."

Ben exhaled. "Nor have I," he admitted. "Forgive me. You are welcome here."

The muscle in Kael's jaw relaxed, and he didn't quite smile, but he nodded, and when he stepped forward to take Ben's outstretched hand, he moved as if he were no longer so broken down.

He didn't look at Briand as he warmed his hands at the fireside after, but she felt his attention on her all the same. He spoke to the woman who brought him stew, his voice a low smudge of sound against the crackle of the flames.

Briand stood and moved away into the shadows at the back of the cave, choosing a place where she could look up and see the night sky through one of the hollows that opened the cave to the outside world. She felt his presence rather than heard it. He sank down beside her, and she didn't look. She ran a finger along her knife's dull side, sorting through her emotions.

"Ben says you bargained information for supplies," he said.

She pulled up her knees to her chest and rested her chin on them. Overhead, one of the stars glittered like a gem caught by candlelight. "Seemed like a good idea."

Their words from before, the ones they'd exchanged like arrows, hurt like fresh wounds. She wanted to spill out words and explanations. She wanted to ask questions. She didn't. She kept the words and explanations all inside, bruised with the need of them.

Whenever she looked at his face, she ached inside. Ached with the way he looked at her like she was a traitor. Ached with the stupid handsomeness of him, and raged that she couldn't ignore it. Why had she never before noticed the stupid jut of his stupid jaw? The way the scar on his face caught the firelight like silver and made her want to touch it?

"I have something to tell you," he said.

Here it was. The rest of it. After he told her, would she tell him her secret, the one she held close as a knife's blade? She licked her lower lip. Her heart thumped against her ribs like a fist on a door.

"We have another mission," Kael said. His eyes were dark and his face half in shadow as he watched her.

Oh.

She was still, parceling her words. "No wonder you rescued me."

He didn't argue; he just held her there with his eyes.

"What mission?" she finally asked, feeling as though she'd lost an argument just by asking the question.

He shook his head. "No details now. But I thought you should know before we reach Yeglorn."

"Yeglorn?" She had heard the name before, dropped carelessly by a traveler in Gillspin at the Dubbok tables, but she knew nothing about it.

"An Estrian city, on the edge of the plains," he explained. "A few days' ride from here. We'll meet the others. Nath, Tibus."

The others. Hope fluttered in her like a wounded bird. The thought of their company, sealed together like family, tight with trust and knit together in loyalty, made the next breath hurt doubly because it was no longer so.

"I'm not a Monarchist," she said, in case he'd forgotten in the last several hours. "I have no plans to become one."

"I know." His voice was soft in the near darkness, all velvet and smoke. "But we need you. The venom made you what you are. You're a part of this, whether you like it or not."

"And you're here to enforce my participation?" She looked up at the stars again.

"I have my orders." He sounded weary. "I don't want to force you to do anything, Briand."

His use of her name made her pulse startle and the tight knot in her chest soften. She was flushed and uneasy, caged with feeling. She closed her eyes and she saw her memory of Kael braced against a tree in the rain, blood pouring from his shoulder.

"I'll go with you to Yeglorn," she said, turning back to face him. "I can promise you that much."

The place between Kael's eyebrows smoothed as he nodded.

She bit her lip and looked back at the stars.

~

Briand dreamed again of Auberon, and once again, they were in the dungeon cell where he had questioned her. She stood with her back against the stone wall and he stood at the bars.

"You're proving more elusive than I thought you'd be," he said. "Even for my Hunters."

"I thought the Hunters were excellent trackers," she said. "I'm just a guttersnipe, and yet they can't find me?"

A frown appeared between his eyebrows. "They cannot seem to get a grasp on your mind." He studied her. "What are you?"

She only laughed at him until she woke.

SIXTEEN

THE DAYS PASSED. Kael healed. Briand practiced throwing her knife at the tapestry on the wall, and after a while, Boot coaxed her into playing Dubbok and lost spectacularly. Ben was a moody thing, but he left them alone, and when the day came that Kael was well enough to ride, Ben kept his promise about the supplies and food, and, to Briand's surprise, horses as well—one a dappled gray gelding that Briand suspected had once belonged to an officer in the prince's army based on the smooth, gliding way he trotted, the other a plain, small brown mare with a streak of black in her mane.

"You're doing me a favor," Ben said gruffly as Boot led the horses out. "That mare will be the death of someone someday. She's stubborn as a stepchild, and she's got the feet and heart of a mountain goat."

"What breed?" Briand asked.

Ben shrugged. "She's a horse."

"She's got tyyrian blood judging by her head and her tail," Kael said, looking the mare over from where he was putting the bridle on the gray. "See how she holds her tail? Like a flag. And Estrian blood, too—see the stripe in her mane, and the faint dark lines near her hooves?"

"She's a mutt," Ben said, dismissive. "A varlet."

If he was trying to dissuade Briand from liking the mare, he was failing miserably. She liked scrappy things. The bridle jingled as the mare shook her mane.

Briand put her hand on the mare's velvety nose, and the horse calmed a little.

Ben muttered something beneath his breath. The mare's ear flicked back to catch the sound of his voice, and she snorted delicately, as if scorning his opinion. A smile crept around the edges of Briand's mouth.

Sunlight streamed through the holes in the ceiling of stone, a waterfall of gold that brought with it the sound of birdsong and trees rustling in the wind. A sliver of shivery blue sky winked between the waving branches. Something in the air made Briand's blood feel hot and restless. Ben bid them a wary farewell, and she mounted and rode in a small circle while Kael and Boot exchanged goodbyes with the clasp of a hand. Then Kael swung himself into the saddle and spurred his horse to a canter. Briand let the mare loose after him, and they flew from the cave into the forest and a shock of green-gold sunlight and shadow.

~

Auberon stood on the bank of the Jessu River at the place where it left the forests and fanned into the upper delta of Sythra's green plains, watching the water flow past as the stench of the mud sucking at his boots filled his nose. The recent floodwaters had uprooted swaths of trees and coated the rocks and bushes in mud. The horses snorted behind him as he took his time scanning the landscape, and he heard a soldier mutter under his breath, but he ignored these ambient noises while he drew in another breath filled with the stink of mud and river water and tried to puzzle out where the fugitives he sought might have gone.

They'd vanished after a brief appearance in Lanternglorn, and they hadn't reappeared in any of the towns downriver. He'd searched every flea-infested inn and tavern between Lanternglorn and Sythra.

A whirring sound whined high in the air, growing closer. As he lifted his head to look, a mechbird dropped from the clouds and landed on his arm. Heat rose from it as it dropped a rolled scroll into his hand.

A golden seal glittered as he turned it over.

It was from the Citadel.

This must be his summons to return.

Auberon clenched his fist around the scroll as the mechbird spread its wings to rise. He grabbed the legs of the thing and threw it down in the mud. One swift stomp broke the delicate gears inside and smashed the mechanical guts across the ground.

If the bird did not return, they could not know that he'd received the summons. It would buy him a little time.

The soldiers behind him wisely remained silent as he returned to his horse with the summons in his hand.

He would find her before he returned.

~

Briand and Kael rode for hours through the forest, down the side of the mountain and into a narrow canyon where a river had worn a passage edged with moss and ferns and paved with river pebbles rounded by the tongue of the water. The river flowed at the bottom of the gully, barely a trickle around the horses' hooves, but a skittish feeling prickled through Briand's fingers and wound around her stomach as she looked at that water and remembered the raging force of the Jessu as it smashed their boat against the rocks. A flash flood would sweep them away.

Finally, they reached the end of the canyon and climbed a bank of crumbling stone. The mare danced up it easy, her hooves finding every groove and crack. She reached the top first and whinnied, the sound carrying triumphantly over the canyon below.

The forest breathed and whispered around them as the sun began to sink. Flowers unfurled in the growing darkness, their petals luminously white. The musical calls of night creatures echoed. A damp chill hung in the air, seeping to her bones, and Briand was grateful to dismount and find wood for a fire.

They holed up in a space where three massive stones rested together like toys abandoned by a giant's offspring. She realized two of the stones were carved faces, one weeping, the lips curved down in sorrow and the eyes closed, the other smiling to reveal teeth blackened with moss and lichen.

Briand unsaddled the horses while Kael coaxed a flame from a pile of kindling and fed it sticks, building the flickering fire until it illuminated the shelter and warmed the back of Briand's neck as she stored the tack beneath an alcove of stone. She found jerky and bread in the saddlebags, and then they ate, he on one side of the fire with his back to mossy stone, she on the other, her shoulders and head resting on the mare's saddle.

"Where are we?" she asked when she'd finished eating and her hands felt restless and empty. Absurdly, she wanted to curl into Kael and nestle her head on his shoulder. She crossed her arms over her chest.

"Less than a day's ride to the border between Tasnia and Estria," Kael said. He stared into the fire. "I used to hunt in these woods with my father as a boy. He liked to make a competition of it between my brother and me, to see who could return with the most hares and doves." He was silent a moment, lost in his thoughts.

Briand had a feeling that these competitions were not so friendly.

Kael looked at her with half of a smile, and stupidly, it made her stomach flip over. "I once took shelter in this very place, although I was a good bit smaller then, so I hid in the mouth of that head." He pointed at the face behind her. "I was waiting for a doe, and it began to rain, and I fell asleep and returned empty-handed." He shook his head.

She was drawn into his tale in spite of herself. "And then what happened?"

Kael's expression closed up a little. "My father whipped me."

She felt ill. "How old were you?"

"I was seven."

The sounds of the forest echoed around them—the staccato cry of some animal Briand couldn't identify, the throaty song of frogs. One of the horses snorted softly in the darkness, and moths fluttered above their heads, wings flashing like bits of moonlight. One brushed her cheek, its wing soft as a snowflake.

He reached for a stick and poked at the embers, stirring sparks into the air. Briand noticed his hands, long and slender—assassin hands, she thought. She could imagine them holding a blade as easily as a quill or an instrument. She let her gaze shift from his hands to his face, marked by shadows, his features unreadable as always but more weary than stern. She remembered how ruthlessly he ran her uncle's estate as steward, the way he'd worn his persona of a bookish man to disguise his true self, or at least the bit of it she'd seen. She felt grudging, bitter admiration.

"I have better memories," he offered then, as if sensing her melancholy. "Once when I was a little older, I found a pit and covered it with brush. My brother trod right across it."

Kael's grin was so infectious she almost returned it before she caught herself. No, Briand thought furiously, he would not endear himself to her with anecdotes of childhood.

"I managed to win that round," Kael said.

"You didn't win usually?" She found that surprising. It was Kael, after all.

His laugh was a faint, startled exhalation. "I never did."

And yet again, he'd surprised her. She straightened against the rock where her lower back had gone numb.

He didn't say anything else about his past. The fire burned lower, but the heat never wavered in its warm radius, and she wondered if he'd whispered something to the coals to keep the flames hot.

Before long, her eyelids drooped, and Kael said he'd take the first watch. She curled up on her bedroll and slept.

~

"You're making this difficult," dream Auberon told her as she slept. "But you will not escape me. I have my Hunters scouring Tasna as far as the Sythran border."

She laughed. "And we're about to pass into Estria. You won't find us there."

The dreams were clearer than any others she had, the details sharp. She could almost feel his breath on her face as he laughed. But she knew she was asleep. If she wanted, she could wake up.

"Then I will come to Estria," he snarled.

"Try to capture me. I'll stab you myself," she said, and then she woke.

~

As they continued their journey, the lush forest thinned into intermittent clearings of yellow grass and fragrant purple flowers that grew so tall the blossoms brushed the bellies of the horses. The scent of them made Briand feel drunk. The mare nipped at the petals, scattering them like raindrops as she pulled her head up.

The land smoothed from the hilly, uneven terrain of the forest to flatter footing. The sun shone warmer, and the air had the feel of silk.

"We're almost to Estria," Kael said at one point. His voice had a current of longing in it that made her look at him twice.

"You're from Tasglorn, yes?" she asked.

"My family's estate is there," he said. "But I spent most of the childhood on our lands in Estria."

She knew a little about Estria, mostly that it was flat and grassy, the domain of horse breeders and cattle ranchers and nomadics.

They reached a stream that cut across the landscape like a ribbon of silver. The mare bent her neck to drink. Kael tossed Briand the canteen, and she gulped a mouthful of cold water. It was tranquil here, with the birdcall echoing around them and the scent of trees and stones hanging in the air. The sun warmed her face, and she wished she could curl up on the sand beside the river, shut her eyes, and forget about Seekers and dragonsaying and Monarchists forever.

The mare put one hoof in the stream, as if testing to see if Briand was paying attention. Briand tugged at the reins absently.

"Ho, Varlet," she said.

Kael looked at her, his eyes, as always, in shadow. She never could tell what he was thinking. "You named the mare?"

"Ben's the one who called her a varlet. I think it suits her." Briand stroked the mare's neck where the black stripe in her mane fell across it. "She's a patchwork of bloodlines and colors. A mutt. She's a good horse for a guttersnipe."

"I think anyone who calls that horse a mutt underestimates her," Kael observed.

Briand shrugged one shoulder. "Like I said, a good horse for a guttersnipe." She grinned at him, forgetting herself for a moment, feeling the sun on her back and the smile on her mouth and the velvet of Varlet's neck under her palm.

Kael's expression changed—his mouth was soft, almost smiling, and his eyes were clear and warm. In that moment, it did not feel so stupid that she cared about him.

Then a branch snapped in the underbrush behind them, and a voice snarled, "Don't move."

SEVENTEEN

BRIAND YANKED HER knife out and whirled Varlet around to do battle. A man stood in the trees behind them, holding a bow, the arrow nocked and drawn. Tension shimmered through her muscles, begging her to let the dagger fly straight at his throat. Kael flicked a finger at her from beside his leg, telling her to wait.

"Get down off your... Kael?" The man lowered the bow. "Is that you? You look like death's leftovers."

Kael laughed. Briand blinked, shocked.

It was Nath.

He was thinner than she remembered, still ugly, his dark hair long and lank, his face too sharp and angular and nervous. He was one of the most beautiful things she'd ever seen. Joy shot through her.

He didn't seem to notice her as he dropped his bow and laughed again. "Kael, you piece of donkey dung. We've been waiting for weeks!"

"And I thought you would have kinder words for us after all this time," Kael remarked, dismounting and striding to meet him halfway between the trees and the stream. Nath clasped his arms in a fierce greeting, and then they embraced. Briand stayed on the mare.

A crashing sound came from her left, and then Tibus burst into the clearing holding a battle axe and shouting a guttural cry that cut short as he spotted his leader and Nath standing together, Nath's bow lowered. He dropped the axe.

"Sir," he said. "We didn't—"

"We thought you were soldiers," Nath said. He tucked the arrow back in his quiver and tapped the end of the bow against Kael's chest. "You're wearing Seeker dubs and riding a soldier's horse. And your companion..."

He looked more closely at Briand and then his eyes widened. "It's the guttersnipe!"

She dismounted and gave a hesitant nod.

Nath strode to her side and grabbed her by the elbows. "You're taller. You look like you've been dragged through a river."

"I'm not as ugly as you, old man," Briand retorted.

Nath cackled. "Still have that vexing spirit, I see." He hugged her.

Tibus approached them. "It *is* you," he said. "I can hardly believe it." He knocked Nath aside to grab her in a bear hug, squeezing her until her ribs protested.

When he set her down, Briand scanned the trees, sudden alarm seizing her. "Where's Bran?"

Nath and Tibus exchanged a glance. Panic made a fist in her stomach. She made a hoarse sound.

"He's on the coast," Tibus said, seeing her distress. "He's not dead, my girl, don't fret."

"He's handling some business for the prince," Nath said. "He gets to sip spiced wine and eat sweetmeats while we comb the wilderness for this renegade." He pointed at Kael. "We've been waiting for you for too long. Weeks. We'd almost given up hope."

"I had a few setbacks in the plan," Kael said, calm and unreadable as always.

"Is she one of the setbacks?" Nath demanded. He jerked his head at Briand, but he was grinning.

"She is part of the plan," Kael said.

Nath made an approving sound. "I'm near famished," he said. "We should get back to the camp before we discuss this further." But he looked to Kael for confirmation. Already, he had shifted into the role of follower.

Kael swung back into the saddle. "Lead the way."

~

Tibus and Nath had established their camp in a hollow behind a waterfall. Droplets sprayed Briand as she climbed the rocks to access the narrow cave. The rushing sound of the water muffled their footsteps and Nath's excited chatter, which was occasionally punctuated by Tibus's grunts or monosyllabic responses. Kael was a quiet murmur.

She felt as though she'd tumbled into a dream. She'd imagined finding them again hundreds of times in the last several years, although mostly she'd imagined slapping Kael across the face, or challenging him to a duel of swords and winning, or pinning his cloak to the wall with her knife before she demanded answers for his abandonment. In her version, Bran was always there along with the others. Reality was surprising, disorienting. But at the same time, she felt safe in a way she hadn't since they'd gone away.

She was unmoored without her touchstone of righteous anger, lost instead in a thorny wood of conflicting feelings. She busied herself sorting the supplies while Tibus laid out a fire and Nath readied a meal.

"We've seen dozens of Cahan's men in this wood," Nath reported as he carved up potatoes for the pot in the fire. "Scouts, spies, even a troop of soldiers."

Kael questioned him about their movements as Briand found a stone to settle on near the fire. Tibus looked at her and smiled, but didn't speak. His face was relaxed, his expression serene, but he wore an air of readiness like a cloak, and he kept one ear tipped toward the entrance.

Neither Tibus nor Nath asked exactly how Kael and Briand fell into company with each other. In fact, they left the matter entirely alone.

"We encountered Ben and his group," Kael said while they ate.

"And how did that go?" Tibus muttered.

"Better than expected." Kael took a bite of bread. "He did try to kill me."

Nath made a sound between a snort and a chortle. "I imagine it didn't go well for him."

Tibus, however, didn't seem to find it funny. "You're in danger, sir," he said. "Rumors abound about your loyalty. If Ben—a friend and fellow—doesn't believe you're a Monarchist at heart, what will your enemies in Jehn's court think?"

Kael didn't answer that.

Beyond the cave, over the sound of the waterfall, a howl split the gathering darkness. They ate quickly and unceremoniously, with the ease of people who'd spent a long time together. Briand, despite her labyrinth of emotions, was struck by how natural it felt to be among them and part of the group again. She wanted to hate it, to fight it, but she instead felt herself thawing, just a little, especially when Nath caught her eye and winked, or Tibus told a joke and laughed harder than anyone else, or when Kael's lips curled around the edges in the smile he had when he was composing a rejoinder. She didn't join in their conversation, but she soaked it in while she ate.

When the meal was finished, Kael and Nath conversed quietly while Tibus banked the fire and put away the food. After a while, Nath pulled a worn pack of Dubbok cards from his pack and tipped his head at Briand. She watched him deal and picked up her hand.

"Shall we make a wager?" he asked.

"Only if you are foolish enough to think you can win. I've only grown better at this game in my absence," she said.

Nath laid down a card. "As the poet says, boasts are usually followed by blushes." He was chuckling.

"If that were true, you'd be forever red," Tibus said.

Laughter made her bladder ache. She held up a finger. "Before I make mincemeat of you, where do you, ah, use the privy?"

"Ah," Nath teased. "You just want to stall for time." He nodded toward the door. "Be sure to go down the river a ways. We drink from it."

"Don't be crass, Nath," Tibus rumbled from his place at the fire as Briand set down her cards and crossed to the cave's entrance.

Outside, the sound of frogs chorused around her. She pushed through the bushes and found a quiet place several dozen yards from the cave. When she was finished, she crept to the water's edge and took a moment to splash water on her face and comb her fingers through her hair before braiding it.

No reason to look like a complete savage now that they were safe.

A sudden foreboding tripped along her spine. The frogs had fallen silent. Briand lowered herself into the reeds and held her breath.

A movement at the place where the forest began gave him away.

A Hunter.

Her heart fell like a stone as he saw her. He lifted his arm, calling a weapon into his hand. She tripped over a stone and fell backward into the water as a hiss swept past her cheek. A whisset?

Bubbles exploded around her in the shock of cold, and then she was being swept into the swirling current, carried along underwater. She fought the cold wet darkness, lungs aching, arms bruising as she hit the rocks. She slammed into something hard and scrambled for a hold. The rock was slippery as ice as she clawed her way up it and into the air.

That first breath was fire.

She made it to shore across a bridge of river rocks. She was bleeding when she fell onto the muddy edge of the river. The Hunter was gone. She crawled into the reeds and lay still, listening for voices, trying not to cough.

Finally, when the frogs began to sing again, she dared to move.

She was halfway back to the cave when hands grabbed her. She fought, but it was Kael's voice saying her name.

"There's a Hunter," she whispered.

"I'll meet you back at the cave." He slipped into the darkness.

When she entered the cave, Tibus and Nath drew her to the fire and dropped a blanket over her shoulders. She recounted the events hoarsely as they listened, Tibus shaking his head and Nath muttering.

They waited for half an hour, tense and worried, and then Kael was back, appearing from the dark like a summoned ghost, soaking wet. He sank down by the fire. "Hunters," he said. "Two of them. And," he hesitated. "With them, one of the Seekers I traveled with. Auberon."

Briand went cold to her fingertips.

"They headed south," Kael said. "I erased your footprints, dragonsayer, in case they return this direction."

"Mercy," Nath muttered.

Kael shook his wet hair and pulled off his wet shirt to wring it out. Droplets clung to his eyelashes and slid down his chest over his scars. His dark hair stuck to the back of his neck and to his temples, and it made his eyes look brighter, sharper, and his cheekbones more angular. He glistened in the firelight.

"We'll leave in the morning for Estria," he said. "They will expect us to continue down the Jessu toward the Monarchist stronghold in Sythra, no doubt. They're looking for a group of two on foot. We'll lose them when we cross. Don't worry."

He might as well have told Briand not to breathe.

In her dream, she'd told Auberon they were headed to Estria.

She couldn't shake the fear that it had been more than a dream.

They settled down, Tibus banking the fire, Nath laying out bedrolls. Briand curled into a ball and tried to sleep. But her heart beat too, and her thoughts were restless.

Tibus snored softly from the other side of the fire, his body only visible as a shadowy hill of shoulder and back. Kael and Nath stayed awake, speaking too softly to understand, their posture curved toward each other, their conversation carrying the cadence of two people who know each other's minds as well as their own.

She shut her eyes and kept them shut until sleep claimed her.

~

In the dream this time, Auberon paced before the bars like a cat, his whole body strung with tension. She became aware of the cell slowly, as if she were waking from sleep instead of the other way around. She struggled to her feet as he turned toward her.

"I almost had you," he hissed. "You slipped right through our fingers."

She watched as he raged. Foreboding grew like a knot beneath her ribs.

"How did you know where to look?" she whispered. As if this dream might tell her the mind of the enemy.

He stopped and looked at her. His eyes narrowed. "Because you told me," he said, as if putting something together. "I had the inkling to search the border because of a dream like this one, in which you said..."

She was afraid. "No," she said.

He shook the bars as she shrank back. "Where are you?"

She didn't understand. She was asleep. She was dreaming. She wasn't within his reach, and he couldn't read her mind anyway.

Was she going mad?

He reached for the door to the cell, but it was bound with a great chain, and he had no key. He dropped the chain with an exclamation of disgust and she breathed easier. He couldn't touch her.

"I will find you," he promised.

"This is a dream," she said firmly, and then she woke.

EIGHTEEN

THE LAKE STRETCHED before Briand like a sheet of silver the next morning, rippling in the wind as the company of Monarchists and dragonsayer stood at the edge, water lapping at their feet. A dock reached over the water, with a house perched at the end and a ferry drawn up beside it.

"We're taking the horses?" Briand asked, a hand on Varlet's neck and a note of worry in her voice.

"Yes," Kael said, his eyes on the horizon. "We'll need them for the trip to Yeglorn."

The dream hung in her mind, dark and heavy with its implications, and she was twisted in knots thinking about it. But in the sunlight, with Kael and the others at her side, she felt safer.

They hadn't been found. It was only a dream.

The house was owned by a one-eyed man, the ferry operator. He ushered them inside and accepted the coins Kael handed him as payment. He grunted something about the wind and the weather before vanishing out into the brightness.

The house was small, the floor uneven, the walls punctuated with windows of a dozen different sizes, some round, and some rectangle. A fireplace smoked in the corner. An old woman sat in a rocking chair beside it, a pipe clenched in her mouth and a snarl of yarn in her hands, humming. She stood when they entered and shuffled to the fireplace to withdraw a kettle. She poured four cups of tea and set them on the table.

The old woman pointed a finger. "Drink," she commanded.

The men meekly picked up the cups. Briand felt a stab of amusement to see these hardened soldiers cradling teacups in their hands, their stances wary even as they sipped the steaming liquid.

The old woman whirled to Briand. "Drink." She squinted, and then ambled forward, her forehead bunching as she reached out a hand. Their fingers met.

Briand pulled back, and the woman stopped, her hand outstretched, her fingers curled. She reached again, and this time Briand didn't move, and the woman cupped her face with age-gnarled fingers and murmured a single word, so quiet it was almost indistinguishable from the slap of water against the bottom of the house.

"Dragonsayer."

Briand was struck immobile. How could she know?

Kael and Nath exchanged a glance.

The woman ran her thumb over Briand's cheekbone, the movement gentle, almost stroking. She made a sing-song noise in her throat, and Briand expected to feel revulsion or skittishness from being touched by this strange old crone, but instead, she felt warmed. Seen. Wanted.

The woman dropped her hand and went back to the fire. The others remained by the door, stunned to silence.

The ferry operator returned with a basket of bread in his arms. "Sit, sit. Eat, eat. We go when the wind is better. When the wind is better."

He repeated everything, the ferry operator. He bustled around the room, humming under his breath, and it was a different song from the one the old woman had hummed. Briand sneaked a look at her; she had hunched into her rocker like a bird perched on a branch, her eyes fixed on the fire.

~

Yeglorn was bursting with color. The city sat on a low hill in the middle of the plain, with a sweep of farmland around it and a silver snake of river curving around city and farmland both like a scythe. Men and women labored in green rows planted alongside the river. Paddocks held striped and spotted horses grazing in herds. The walls of the city fluttered with flags that flapped and danced in the wind in hundreds of color combinations, and the gates to the city were painted blue.

A smaller gate set in the larger ones opened to admit them, and the group dismounted to enter the city, leading the horses behind. Briand gazed around her in wonder.

Every single door in the city was painted the color of the sky. Gently sloping roofs covered in grass held grazing livestock or drying laundry. The streets were packed dirt swept clean.

They passed a marketplace swarming with men and women dressed in muted browns and golds, hands covered in fingerless leather gloves, their waists cinched with sashes and tooled leather belts hung with knives and ropes. Many of the women wore riding trousers instead of skirts, and their hair curled around their heads or down their backs in braids bound with strips of cloth. Everyone wore boots, even the woman in a fine pink dress that Briand saw choosing fruit from a stall in the market while her attendant held a parasol over her head.

In a plaza just beyond the marketplace, a crowd of people had gathered restlessly around a platform of splintered wood. Atop the platform stood a man, shirtless, his head bowed and his hands bound in front of him, fingers splayed across a block of wood. As they rode past, a man in black lifted an axe and swung it down across the man's right hand. Blood splattered the cobblestones. The man made a sound like a gutted animal.

"Punishment for crimes against the prince," a soldier called out as the man continued to scream. "Let all who see take note."

Nath muttered something under his breath. "One day, that could be us," he said to Kael.

"Chopping off fingers? They'll take off our heads," Kael replied. His face was expressionless, but his eyes were troubled as he turned them away from the man on the platform.

Finally, the company reached a tall, narrow house with a courtyard and a pair of heavy blue doors with brass handles in the shape of horses' heads. Kael knocked, and a guardsman stepped out to inquire his name before the doors opened to admit them to a courtyard.

A man in pale brown robes edged with gold stood in the center of the courtyard, waiting. He was perhaps twice Kael's age, his beard threaded with gray. He clasped hands with Kael, and they put their heads together a moment, murmuring a greeting only they could hear. Then the man turned to the rest of them.

"The House Barria welcomes you," he said. His gaze came to rest on Briand, his expression curious. "I am Lord Barria. Please come."

Servants took the horses' reins, and they followed Lord Barria inside. The polished stone floors were bare of rugs, and the walls were covered with wood carvings and stitched tapestries. Candles lit the rooms with a warm glow instead of the harsh light of electric power.

"May the true prince sit on the throne," Barria murmured once they were indoors. He clasped one fist across his chest, and Tibus and Nath thumped their arms in a similar gesture, murmuring the same fervently. Briand said nothing, which Lord Barria did not miss. His eyebrows curved, but he only said, "Servants will show you to your rooms. Don't worry— all my people are loyal to the death."

A woman dressed in a plain tunic with loose trousers peeking from underneath the hem showed Briand to her quarters, a room draped in curtains with a wall of windows overlooking the courtyard below. A bed piled with pillows and sheepskin blankets stood in the middle of the space, and Briand wanted to sink into it and sleep for days. But the servant informed her that she was to wash for dinner and meet the others below in the garden for the meal.

Briand bathed and dressed in clean clothing provided by the servant before going in search of the others.

They dined in a garden with a stone fountain in the center.

The servants had laid out plates and utensils. The others were already present, along with the Lord Barria and his family.

Lord Barria rose.

"May I present my wife, Alis, and my children, Sobin and Cait." A woman with dark eyes and skin the color of coffee nodded demurely in greeting. Beside Alis sat a young man with full, pouty lips and eyes fringed by long lashes, and a girl on the cusp of womanhood, slender as a gazelle, her hair a cascade of curls and her smile a promise of a smirk. They both nodded in greeting, miniatures of their mother. Briand inclined her head stiffly before taking her seat between Kael and Nath.

Two cats lazed beneath the fountain. They were the size of dogs, their ears long and tufted, their tawny coats spotted and their tails marked with faint stripes. They blinked slitted golden eyes at Briand, and one yawned, exposing its teeth. They both wore jeweled collars that glittered as they stood and twined toward her.

One of the cats rubbed against Lord Barria's chair, and he dropped a hand to its head. "This is Eso, and that is his sister, Isa." He nodded at the second cat, which stretched herself across the ground behind Cait's chair. "They are domesticated sand cats, and they serve as guard animals as well as pets."

Eso fixed his eyes on Nath and yawned, exposing his curved teeth. Nath clutched a napkin to his chest in horror.

"They won't hurt you," Cait spoke up. "Don't fear. They're both just lazy babies, really."

Nath sniffed. "Lazy babies with teeth like scythes." He kept a careful eye on both cats.

The meal was a mixture of grains and vegetables, lightly spiced. Alis and Lord Barria served everyone themselves after the servants brought the food to the table.

Briand recoiled at the inclusion of roasted locusts on a platter with a red sauce drizzled over the twiggy bodies, but no one else batted an eye when the server plopped the dish onto the table. Briand watched as the lady placed two of the locusts on her plate. She caught Kael watching her with amusement. She straightened and picked up one of the locusts resolutely.

Something muscular and silky-soft bumped against her leg. Isa, the sand cat. Briand dropped her hand, offering the locust to the cat under the table. She felt the rough brush of the cat's tongue against her fingers as Isa took it.

The lord made polite small talk while the food was served. He spoke of the six foals that had been born recently to his herd, and his plans for buying a new stallion from Tyyr to breed with his Estrian mares. "I hear it makes for fine, hardy horses."

"Briand rides a mare that is a mixture of Tyyrian and Estrian stock," Kael said. "Perhaps something else as well."

"Oh?" Lord Barria looked intrigued. "How is her temperament?"

"Feisty," Briand said. She'd almost been caught feeding the second locust to Eso, who had joined his sister at her chair beneath the table and who was currently sniffling at her knees for more food. "She's fast, small, and she climbs rocks like a goat."

"She might have a little Bestani pony blood in her, then. They are small, usually no more than fourteen hands high, and I've seen one scale the crumbling part of the city wall like a spider once." It was Cait who spoke. Her cheeks flushed a little when Kael and Briand looked at her.

"Scale the city wall?" Briand felt a rush of scorn for this pampered lord's daughter pretending to know anything about horses. "Are you sure you weren't watching a mountain goat from a distance?"

"It was a Bestani," Cait said firmly. "I know them. I've made a study of the breeds." Color flamed in her cheeks.

"Cait is very involved with the horses," Lord Barria offered. "She's been visiting the stables since she was a small child."

Briand held back a snort. Her uncle had fancied himself involved with his livestock as well. He liked to walk along the stalls, remarking about them as if he knew anything he was talking about. He'd once referred to one of his mules as a Lyponese, a fine breed from the island nation of Messet, and as far from a mule as a housecat from a lion. Briand hadn't been able to contain her giggle when he'd said it. He'd had her punished later for laughing at him in front of the stable hands.

Cait met her gaze, and a hint of a frown formed between her eyes eyebrows.

The cats pressed against Briand's knees beneath the table, and she felt the rumble of their purrs. When she offered no more food, they stalked back to the fountain and dropped to the ground, tails twitching.

When the dinner was finished, servants cleared the places. Lord Barria laid his hands on the table, palms down, and his face grew somber.

"We must discuss the future, my friends." He stopped. His wife and children rose and departed without a word. The servants vanished into the house. Briand started to stand, for this was Monarchist business, but Kael's fingers wrapped around her wrist.

"Stay," he said. "This involves you." He looked at the others. "It is time to discuss the plan."

NINETEEN

KAEL STOOD AND scanned the faces around the table. "The prince and his cabinet are close to securing the alliance between the true prince and the queen of Nyr," he said.

"The Serpent Queen?" Lord Barria's brows rose. "But Nyr never makes alliances."

"This queen might," Kael said. "But her advisors are demanding proof of our loyalty to her and against Bestane."

Little was known in Austrisia regarding the new queen of Nyr. Even among the nobility, stories were scarce—mostly how she was young and unproven, the only daughter of the unpopular king of the House of the Serpent, who'd died from an assassination after he acted indecisively in a long, brutal war. He understood Lord Barria's surprise.

Nath looked at the dragonsayer, who was stiff in her chair, perhaps unwilling to admit confusion. "Nyr and Bestane are mortal enemies," he explained. "If Nyr sides with Prince Jehn, it will be because Bestane is already allied with the usurper prince, that bastard Cahan—and because the queen knows she will need allies when Bestane grows hungry for her islands again. Bestane attacked twenty years ago under her father's reign. It was a bloody war with heavy losses for Nyr, although Bestane was driven back. Now, with the new queen, Bestane seeks to take what they tried and failed to take before," Nath said.

Briand nodded. "It was spoken about in the thief-queen's den by those who cared about such things," she said.

"Cahan thinks Nyr is inconsequential," Kael continued. "He believes the queen will be easily overpowered, thus he allied himself with Bestane and their mighty military. Bestane's emperor has a fleet of ironclad warships, and spies tell us he is gathering his army to strike. Nyr must be able to defend themselves against Bestane."

"Does the true prince believe Nyr capable of fending off such an attack?" Lord Barria asked. "If we invest our dwindling resources courting the aid of the queen and she is not capable—"

"She is capable," Kael said. "She only needs to prove herself."

He'd seen so himself a year ago, before he'd gone on his mission as a traitor. The queen was the shrewdest ruler he'd ever seen, despite her cultivated aura of innocence. He'd reported as much to Jehn.

"And what does this have to do with the guttersnipe, of all people?" Nath waved a hand at the dragonsayer.

"The Serpent Queen seeks to build cannonry and ships to defend her islands against Bestane. She needs funding, and the delicate political situation in her country means she cannot gain it through taxes. She walks a fine line with her advisors. She wants the prince to pledge his support by providing the funds to build her defenses."

"And how much does this queen think the true prince can give her?" Nath demanded. "Cahan has all the palaces, all the carriages and airships. We have, what, a few strongholds and the loyalty of a handful of barons? What is she asking for?"

"Half a million dubois," Kael said.

Lord Barria raised his eyebrows even higher.

"Half a million. Half a *million?*" Nath choked on a laugh, eyes wide in disbelief, his cup sloshing as he set it down. "That's an emperor's ransom. A *rich* emperor's ransom. We sleep in trenches of mud, and she thinks he's got half a million to build her cannons with? She is as foolish as they say if she thinks she can secure anything approaching that from him. Bestane knows it. Cahan knows it. Has wind of this negotiation gotten out? It will ruin her. She is obviously desperate to the point of madness as it has been rumored—"

"Word has gotten out," Kael interrupted crisply. "As spies are rampant among her councilmembers and court, and nearly every word is listened to through cracks in the walls and holes in the grates. However, she is not as foolish as you might think. Cahan will laugh, and Bestane will scheme, but the prince intends to deliver this to her, and more."

"More?" Tibus spoke with a low rumble.

Kael only smiled.

"What is your plan?" Lord Barria asked.

"And why do you need a dragonsayer?" Nath pointed at Briand.

He paused. He was about to test their commitment with his next words. "Does the treasure of Jaseel mean anything to any of you?" Kael asked.

They were silent, except for Nath's intake of breath.

The dragonsayer stirred. "What is the treasure of Jaseel?"

"A myth," Nath said, his mouth pulling down into a worried scowl.

"We've dealt with myths before," Kael said. "Why not now?"

No one had an answer for him. Tibus looked shaken, Lord Barria troubled.

"Tell me," Briand said.

"King Belgru the Golden, ruler of Austrisia in the Old Time, hid a vast treasure beneath his southern estate," Kael said, speaking directly to Briand now. "The treasure is rumored, as Nath is correct in saying, to be worth more than two million dubois. It rightfully belongs to Prince Jehn, although I'm sure the usurper prince would beg to differ. But neither has it in his possession, at least not yet. It's said to be in a cave in the southeast of the southern province."

"If such a vast fortune is real," Briand said, a skeptical frown on her face, "then how is it possible that no one has taken it before now?"

"Because everyone who's ever tried doesn't come back—" Nath began.

"Because," Kael finished, "the treasure is guarded by dragons."

Even Lord Barria's eyes widened slightly.

The dragonsayer leaned forward. Her long brown hair brushed her shoulders. "So... we walk in, I hold off the dragons, the rest of you snatch the treasure?"

"Well, it isn't so simple," he said. "The location of the treasure rests below what is now the estate of Cahan's chief physician, Aron Kul."

"The Butcher of Tasglorn," Tibus muttered. He rubbed his arm. "He is said to cut off arms and legs just for the pleasure of it. He's said to carve skin from faces, make tatters of lips and noses."

Kael didn't deny it.

"His estate is known for its impassibility," he continued. "Moats, pits, traps, snares. He has a labyrinth of stone in his gardens, and poisoned vines growing on the estate walls. He keeps an entire orchard of bloodtrees, the most poisonous plant known to man. He's a paranoid man with sick fascinations, and his decorating reflects this."

"If you're trying to convince us of the feasibility of this..." Nath muttered.

"I don't want anyone to be under the illusion that this will be easy," Kael said. He gazed at each of them in turn, searching their expressions for doubt or fear. "However, on my last mission, I obtained detailed sketches of the inside grounds. We won't be operating blindly."

"What's our plan for sneaking inside?" Tibus asked.

Kael tipped his head. "We're going to walk through the front gate, disguised as guests."

Tibus scowled. "Disguised," he said, as if he'd rather hack his way through a horde of dogs. "As *guests.*"

"Guests of what?" Nath asked. "Kul's latest bloody experiment?"

"It seems Lord Kul is seeking a wife," Kael said. "It's rumored he had a bit of a nervous collapse that led to his leaving Tasglorn for Sythra, and now that he's living at a slower pace, he wants to settle down. He's hosting his birthday celebration and rumor has it that pretty, well-connected women are more than welcome. I've already sent a missive requesting an invite."

They all looked at Briand, who flushed.

Tibus cleared his throat. He chose his words with the care. "Do you really think the dragonsayer is the best choice for this, er, most delicate of tasks?"

Nath was blunter. "I've never seen her flirt, mind you, but I have no doubt she has the sensitivity of a rabid dog. She'll knife the man as soon as look at him."

"Briand will play the part of a handmaiden," Kael said. "I am not void of sense. Maera will play the suitor."

"Maera," Nath remarked tonelessly.

Nath didn't like Maera.

"She joins us in a few weeks." He slid back his chair and stood. "Until then, we prepare ourselves. Learn our parts. Study these plans and work out the best system for once we've gained access. We must be flawless in our execution of each step."

As they departed the garden, he caught Briand by the elbow. Her eyes were bright with something he couldn't identify as she stared up at him.

"I saw you feed the locusts to the cats," he said.

~

Auberon came to the entrance to his tent to receive the mechbird. They had an easier time finding him when he was near a town, if the miserable huddle of buildings against the lake could be properly called a town. The bird's gears were hot against his gloved palm as he withdrew the scrolled letter from Jade and unfurled it.

Little Brother,

The matter you inquired about—dream entanglement—is not something I can find much about. The section of the library that was lost to fire years ago may have contained something, but the books I looked through said little on the subject, except that it was reported by a Seeker interrogating a farm girl in the early fourth century after the Schism. It is said that he learned much about the milking of cows from the matter.

This archaic incident is hardly something for you to be concerning yourself with at a time like this.

There was more, but not pertaining to his question. He scanned the rest, and then tucked the letter into his shirt.

One of the Hunters had caught sight of her in the darkness, but she was as elusive to their abilities as she was to his. She'd vanished into the night.

He read over the contents of Jade's letter again.

It is said he learned much about the milking of cows from the matter.

She joked, but perhaps there was something there.

He burned the letter in the campfire.

TWENTY

BRIAND DID NOT dream that night. Still, she woke restlessly at dawn and slipped from her bed in the chilly gray light to brush Varlet until the sun had begun to warm the stones of the courtyard and her nerves were calm. The threat of the dreams, and what they could mean, waited at the edge of her mind like a brewing storm cloud. She told herself they were only dreams, but she didn't know if she believed that. Monarchists, Seekers—she was sleeping on a bed of blades, and one wrong move would leave her gutted.

At breakfast, Kael handed Briand four glass bottles filled with leaves.

"What's this?" she said, looking at the leaves inside. All were reddish-purple and shaped like shriveled arrowheads.

"Three bottles contain harmless plants," he said crisply. "One holds the leaves of the bloodtree, which will cause boils to erupt across your skin on contact. If you inhale the smoke of it as it burns, you will grow dizzy and you might lose consciousness. If the oil touches your eyes, you could go blind. Ingest it, and you will die."

Briand set the bottles carefully on the table. The leaves looked identical. "Which one has the bloodtree leaves?"

"I'm not going to tell you. It is possible to observe the difference, but only from the leaves like these that come from the tops of the trees. In three days' time,

I'll have you choose. We'll burn the others and see if you're correct."

She looked at him, horrified, but he seemed utterly serious. "Our mission's success will depend in part on your knowledge in this. So learn, and learn well."

Nath, who stood at Kael's left hand, handed her a book on botany. "This might help," he said.

She took the book.

~

Cait cornered Briand after breakfast and announced that they would be taking a ride with the sort of confidence Briand soon realized the young woman brought to every endeavor she attempted.

"Kael wants—" Briand began, not because she was particularly determined to follow every order Kael issued, but because it seemed a good excuse.

"Hang that," Cait said, and Briand was so startled she laughed. And then she agreed. She found herself dragged to the stables, where Varlet and a black mare with a spotted face waited for them, already saddled. Cait mounted in a fluid motion and spurred her mount forward, and Briand followed suit. They wove through the city, dodging merchants and soldiers. When they reached the gate, they turned right to exit the city and rounded the wall, and Cait drew up sharp.

"Look," she said fiercely, throwing a glance at the wall as she spoke. "It wasn't a mountain goat. I'm not an idiot. I know horses."

"Fine," Briand said, taken aback.

The wind blew curls across the lord's daughter's face and lips. She shaded her eyes with one hand against the sunlight. Her eyebrows drew together, straight and sharp as two arrowheads.

"Do you want to race?" she said.

Briand looked at the stretch of plain before them. The wind teased her hair as it whirled past them and made the long grass dance.

She nodded.

Cait responded by slapping the reins against her mount's neck. Briand spurred the mare after her, and Varlet sprang forward like a doe.

The race was breathless. Briand won by a hair.

When they returned from the ride, windblown and sunburned, Sobin was shooting arrows in the courtyard, the sand cats at his feet, their eyes tracking the arrows as they flew.

"Who won?" he asked without taking his eyes from the target.

Cait swung off her horse. "The little mare is windblessed," was all she said.

Sobin laughed. He let an arrow fly, and it hit the target dead center.

Briand dismounted without speaking. They were like a strange species to her, these secure and confident siblings. They inhabited their world with so much careless, unstudied presence, so much vivacity.

Sobin gave her a sidelong glance as he retrieved his arrows. "Do you know how to shoot, dragonsayer?"

"We aren't supposed to call her that," Cait said, hands on her hips, sounding like the older sister that she was. "Remember?"

"My apologies." He had dimples when he smiled. "Briand, is it?"

"Yes," Briand said carefully. "And no."

Sobin laughed. "You're an economical one. Which reply goes with which question?"

"I've never shot a bow," she said.

"Ah." He notched an arrow and drew his arm back. "Well, come here, and I'll teach you."

His cocky air was easily seen through after her weeks with the inscrutable Kael, but she let him try to use it on her anyway, because she discovered she liked being smiled at, and because he reminded her a tiny bit of Bran, and because Cait was bubbling with laughter as one of the sand cats startled itself with its own tail and then stalked away sulkily to lie in the shade of the columned breezeway.

For that moment, she felt as though everything could be all right.

~

That night, she dreamed the dream again. The cell, the bars. Auberon.

He stood watching her as she became aware of her surroundings. His expression was as sharp as a bayonet, his eyes narrowed and bright with suspicion. She looked at the cell door, and it was still locked. Her eyes flew back to his.

"What was it you told the doctor your name was?"

She was silent, trying to keep her wits about her even in the fog of the dream. Tonight, she had a plan.

"Briand, wasn't it?" He drew out the words with a snarl. "You've had your fun. You've given us a delightful chase and you've proven that you're clever. But it's time to surrender."

She tried to wake herself, but she was stuck in the dream like a fly in a web. She stayed mute.

He rattled the bars again. "This cell seems smaller."

He was right. She noted with dismay that the space between the bars and the wall had shrunk. He could almost reach her if he stretched out his arm. She stepped back to the wall, and Auberon took notice and smiled harshly.

"Tell me where you are, girl. I won't hurt you." He paused. "I'll even let that traitor friend of yours live."

She wasn't stupid. He was lying. She shook her head.

If she was going to do this—plant a false seed of information as a test—she had to play it right. He couldn't know what she was attempting.

He slammed his hands against the bars. "Tell me! Or I'll kill you both when I find you!"

"We're in Eastburn," she cried out.

It was a little town south of Yeglorn.

He smiled. "Was that so hard?"

Then she heard a voice calling her name, and she was wrenched out of the dream and into consciousness. She was drenched in sweat and breathing hard.

Cait stood in the doorway, beckoning to her. "You shouted in your sleep. Wake up, goose. We're going riding."

Briand slid off the bed and pressed a shaking hand to her forehead.

The seed had been planted. Now, she'd see if Seekers came to Eastburn.

Perhaps it was madness. Or perhaps it would confirm what she feared—that she could actually speak with the Seeker in her dreams.

TWENTY-ONE

ESTRIANS WERE STURDY people, grown with a mixture of sun, soil, and sweat. The whole house hummed with busyness from sun up to sun down, a comforting sort of busyness that made Briand feel like a pebble on a beach, surrounded by other pebbles and warmed by the same sun. Although the Lord Barria was a nobleman, he rode out with his men to see to his stock and herd and brand them himself, and his wife worked in the garden and exercised the horses in the paddock. Everyone had a task, and they didn't shirk. Briand's uncle would starve in his receiving hall before working alongside his men in his fields, she thought, watching as Lord Barria dunked his head in a trough after returning home from a dusty ride outside the city. The fading sunlight caught the droplets as they fell from his chin, turning them to beads of fire, and he laughed at something his manservant said to him as he wiped them away with the front of his shirt.

Briand wasn't the only one who felt happier in Estria. She noticed the hungry way Kael looked at the land, as if he thought enough time in this earthy place of wind and sky would heal the things that gave him nightmares in the night.

At night, the Estrians drank gingered beer, threw darts, and played a game with cups and fists that usually ended in someone's knuckles being bloodied. They told raucous stories that had even Nath snorting with laughter. Cait liked to dance, Estrian dances with clasping hands and spinning circles and dizzying footwork that left the dancers breathless when the music ended, and she tried to drag the rest of them into joining her. Kael obliged her, and Briand covertly admired the way he moved, sleek and lean, graceful as a sand cat on the hunt. Cait even managed to cajole Nath into a Tasnian dance, a formal dirge of a movement that Nath exercised grimly as if he were attending a funeral.

When he'd finished, Briand remarked that it looked easy enough, and Kael challenged her to replicate the steps. And so she did, the near darkness hiding the flush on her skin. His hands were warm on her elbows and the night was smooth as a river around them. She'd been lost in a river with him before, in the flood, but this was twice as dizzying. When they were done, she forgot to demand that he acknowledge she'd remembered the steps correctly because her heart was beating in her throat, and she couldn't trust herself to speak coolly enough.

~

Kael holed himself up in Lord Barria's study, sending and receiving correspondence related to the Monarchist rebellion. Letters came in the night through a slit in the gate, or in the morning, the papers tucked into a spare jug slipped in with the fresh milk when it was delivered, or at sunset before they sat down for dinner. Kael was often absent from meals, or distracted, his eyes distant, his expression absorbed in secret thoughts. His moodiness only further exacerbated her emotions, and she alternately found herself withdrawing from him or heatedly sparring with him over the most ridiculous and miniscule details. Kael seemed willing to engage in such arguments when he wasn't distracted, and she was never sure if she felt thrilled or furious that he rose to her goading.

Nath seemed slightly jumpy, but it was Nath, after all, and Briand could not deduce if his demeanor meant anything was amiss or not. He alternately snapped at everyone and holed himself in the library or the study with Kael. Occasionally, Briand heard them arguing in low, tense voices when she passed the closed door.

"What is it?" she asked Tibus at mealtime when Kael looked particularly vexed.

"Seekers," Tibus said. "Our network reported one just arrived at Eastburn this morning."

Briand's lungs lost air. Tibus's voice faded away along with the rest of the hum of the dinner table as she felt herself falling.

It was true, then, what she suspected.

The question now was whether or not she should tell Kael.

TWENTY-TWO

A STORM SWEPT over the plain and enveloped the city, and Briand and Nath were driven inside from sparring, both drenched. The house was nearly deserted, and thunder echoed in the halls. Briand almost collided with Kael as he swept into the hall from the vestibule, water streaming from his hair and dripping down his neck, a traveler's satchel tucked under his arm. A cloak disappearing at the end of the hall suggested he'd gotten the satchel from a visitor, perhaps a Monarchist spy.

She needed to tell him about the dreams.

Kael wiped the rain from his eyes with his wrist. "Sparring?" he asked.

"Nath says he'll teach me knife combat next."

"I've promised nothing of the sort," Nath retorted, shaking water from his hair like a dog as he came out of the downpour. "If you want that sort of instruction, talk to Kael. He's the one who's accustomed to skullduggery."

Kael's eyebrows slashed together. The faintest of smiles touched his mouth at the edges, just a flick of his lips. She almost felt she'd imagined it there. "If you wish," he said to Briand, surprising her. She would have expected a curt refusal.

"You'd trust me to come at you with a knife?" she asked, almost daring him. She wanted to see that smile again, and she didn't know how to get it back.

"I'd easily disarm you."

She pressed her lips together as she studied him. Two years ago she would have boasted about her skill, protested his dismissal loudly. Now she held in the words that immediately leapt to her tongue, seeking through them for the right phrase, the correct tone. She imagined herself as a thief-queen bathed in moonlight. "Perhaps we should have those lessons, just to see."

He cocked his head. No smile, which disappointed her. "Perhaps."

Something about the way he looked at her made her feel flushed and unsettled. She stared after him as he strode away.

"He's only in a mood because he got a letter," Nath said. "Never you mind. It isn't about you, guttersnipe."

The dreams, her mind reminded her.

Briand followed Kael to the library and stopped short just inside. Kael stood with his back to her, his hair dripping water onto the ground as he rubbed a cloth through it. The sound of the door hitting the wall echoed loudly.

Kael turned, the cloth in his hands. When he saw it was her, his expression smoothed over. "What is it?"

"I..." Briand said. She felt exposed, rattled. This was a mistake. What would he do with the knowledge that she was bound to a Seeker through dreams, that she'd already betrayed their location once?

She turned to go as she lost her nerve. She needed to think of a better way to present it before she confessed.

"Wait." He pulled the shirt over his head and picked up a book from the desk before he crossed the room in three steps. "Dragonsayer."

Anger tasted like bile.

"Tibus, Nath, even Cait and Sobin," she said, "you call them all by their names, but I am only Dragonsayer, or Guttersnipe, or Catfoot. We've shared caves and cells together. You've seen me bleed. I've saved your life. Yet I have as much identity as of a piece of sharpened steel to you."

She took the book he held out, a tome on Sythran etiquette, and turned to go. After all this time, she was still just a pawn in the hands of those playing at king making.

He caught her hand. The touch of his fingers was like lightning.

"Wait."

She hesitated at the door. His fingers were still on her wrist.

"This mission..." He stopped, searching her face. "Every person is vital for its success."

She waited for him to continue. Every word she could speak felt monumental. She felt the weight of them all pressing her down.

"I need to know I can trust you," he said.

Did he suspect at what she had come to tell him? Or was it one of her other secrets? Uncertainty lanced her. "We've come this far together, haven't we?"

"I want to talk to you about the Hermit."

Her stomach clenched like a closed fist.

"No," she said, but he reached past her and shut the door.

TWENTY-THREE

"I CAME FOR you, and you were gone," he said. "The cabin was half destroyed, the wall splattered with blood, the Hermit facedown in a puddle of it. Dead. And you were gone."

She breathed in and out slowly. "You abandoned me, and then it was too late. And I was forced to make choices to save myself."

"You ran," he said. His eyes slitted. "The way you always do."

"Always?" Briand shot back. It was as if he'd slapped her. If he was angry, she could match that. The emotions licked along her bones like fire in a dry forest, blazing fast and spitting sparks. She had years of kindling amassed to ignite. "Like when you and the rest of your crew were tied to trees and I cut you free? Like when I called up dragons to destroy your bridge?"

He leaned forward. She leaned forward. They were nose to nose, breathing fury.

"What did you do to the Hermit, Briand?"

She turned her face away. "Nothing."

"You're lying. What are you lying about?"

"You don't know what happened!"

He caught her wrist. "Then tell me."

"I cannot," she said. "And I will not."

There was nothing else to be said, and everything else to be said, but no one would say it. They were silent, Briand imprisoned in all the words she refused to speak, the explanations she wouldn't lay before his scornful examination, the memories in her own mind that circled her like shackles.

~

I did come.

She threw the knife with fury, and it buried itself deep into the edge of the painted burlap target hanging at the opposite end of the practice hall.

The cabin was half destroyed—

She crossed the room in five strides.

Blood splattered with blood—

She yanked the knife free and returned to her place to throw again.

The Hermit facedown in a puddle of it.

She let the knife fly. It hit the edge again.

Dead.

She remembered. The way he'd laid there, like a doll, arms and legs splayed in unnatural angles. The way the blood looked like sap against the wooden walls, dark and viscous. The way her insides felt like broken glass as she'd scrambled back, blood on her hand that she left smeared on the wall.

Blood on the cabin walls. Blood on her hands. Her breath like a startled animal, scrambling in her lungs and throat.

Kael's questions had scared the memories out into the open of her mind, and she couldn't seem to make them go back into hiding.

She'd been a fool to think she could step back into her role among them. A fool to think things hadn't

182

changed irrevocably. A fool to think he'd trust her now.

She was done being a fool.

She wouldn't tell him about the Seeker dreams.

~

Kael waited for her in the library beside shelves of tomes stretching from floor to ceiling and a desk of gleaming flamewood, his shirtsleeves rolled to his elbows and his wrists stained with ink. When she arrived with Nath, he faced her as if he expected a fight on his hands.

"I left instructions with the Hermit to teach you to read and write properly," Kael continued crisply, after another pause. "Did he?"

The mention of the Hermit made her nauseated. She kept her gaze tacked to Kael's. His eyebrows drew together as he waited for her reply.

"He did." She dropped the words into the silence like stones into a well.

"Good," Kael said briskly. "Show us."

He indicated the desk with his hand. A sheaf of papers and a pen lay waiting for her.

She sat.

"Write something," Kael said.

She scrawled her name and held it out. "Is my penmanship pretty enough to pass as a lady's maid?"

He didn't smile. "Is that all you can write?"

Briand picked up the pen and wrote: *Kael is a pompous jackass.*

Nath leaned over to see it. He snickered. "Well, she is literate."

Kael looked at the page. "I see you still act like a guttersnipe."

She set the pen down with a snap. The mood changed to a chill. Nath's grin disappeared as he looked between them.

Kael waited.

Briand bent over the page again. The pen scratched on the paper loudly. After she'd finished, she pushed her chair back and stood.

"I'll be in the courtyard. Nath?"

Nath followed her out, leaving Kael alone with the paper.

~

"He's in a temper," Kael heard Nath say as he and the dragonsayer reached the sunshine-soaked courtyard below. "It isn't your fault, guttersnipe."

Her answer was a murmur lost on the wind.

The clap of hand against wood rang out as Nath tossed the dragonsayer a practice sword. Kael leaned against one of the columns, watching as she pushed a lock of dark hair from her eyes and assumed a fighting position.

He picked up the paper she'd left on the desk.

I didn't kill the Hermit, it read.

He crumpled it into his fist.

~

"The bottles," Kael reminded Briand after a few days, and so she brought them to Lord Barria's study and lined them on his desk. He watched her without saying a word as she set them out, and then he lit a fire in the grate and faced her with his hands clasped. His face was stern as stone, and her stomach made a fist as she stood before him. A storm was brewing at the horizon, and the promise of it stirred her blood.

"What have you learned?" he asked with a nod at the bottles.

I've learned not to trust you, she thought.

She picked up the first, watching his face as she shook it and made the leaves inside rattle. He gave away nothing, not a twitch of an eye or lip. Not a flicker of a finger.

She set it down and trailed her fingertips over the tops of the others before selecting the last one. She lifted it.

"This is the bloodtree," she said, and then she uncorked it and tossed the leaves into the fire.

Kael never flinched.

The leaves melted into a sticky goo over the logs. Briand raised an eyebrow.

"I've learned," she said, "that your bloodtree leaves are wax." She set the bottle down with a thump on the desk.

Kael smiled so faintly she almost missed it. It was a sharp smile, the kind that said he hadn't underestimated her cleverness.

185

"I'd hardly cart such a poisonous substance around simply for educational purposes," he replied. "Very good. And the others?"

"This one," she said with a tap on the first bottle, "is witch's bane. The stems are purple, not red, and the points of the leaves have a yellowish hue. The others are fool's blood and yarblossom. They are too large and too dark to be bloodtree leaves."

"Very good," he said.

His praise startled her. She met his eyes, and he was the one to turn away.

~

This time, when she dreamed the dream, the cell was smaller still. Auberon could put his hands through the bars and almost reach her.

"You weren't at Eastburn," he said. "You are lying to me."

"You'll never find us," she spat, pressing back against the wall.

"I will make you tell me."

"It's only a dream," she said, but she was afraid.

He lunged forward, straining, and his hand caught her wrist. He yanked her forward against the bars. His arm closed around her neck, squeezing tight, and pain blossomed across her neck.

"Tell me," he breathed.

She fumbled for a knife. Did she have a knife? Her fingers closed over steel, and she drew it and slashed him across the forearm. He cried out and dropped her.

She scrambled away, her throat throbbing. The dream began to recede into merciful wakefulness, and she heard the cry of birds in the distance, and the sound of a man saying "Sir. Sir."

She could hear into his world. Could he hear into hers?

Auberon locked eyes with her.

"I will find you," he promised.

When she woke, her throat still ached. She sat up and looked around her at the room. A knock came at the door, and it was Cait, her eyes laughing as she stepped inside.

Briand felt a weary ache down to her bones as she rose from the bed and the knowledge of what she was going to do took shape in her mind.

She was going to run away.

It was the only way she could see to keep everyone safe.

TWENTY-FOUR

BRIAND DIDN'T KNOW when she was going to leave, although she'd already copied several maps from books in Lord Barria's study and hidden them in a slit beneath a leather chair in the library, along with a few other supplies, because she didn't trust Kael not to search her room after his accusations about the Hermit. She'd been adding to it slowly, a coin she'd found in the dirt of the street, a few strips of jerky slipped from the kitchens, a flask of water. Slowly, slowly, so no one, not even sharp-eyed Kael, would notice her preparations. Even as she made them, she wondered if she were mad to imagine not running.

She berated herself for such thoughts immediately. Why did she feel tethered to these people who only wanted to use her to call dragons for them? Who showed her exactly what they thought of her the last time, when they abandoned her with the Hermit? Everything binding her to these people, to this cause, was thin as gossamer, and the dangers were as sharp and deadly as a knife against her throat. She was saving their lives by leaving, not that they would ever know. She was doing the right thing for everyone, including herself.

She was no martyr.

Briand imagined it every night before she slipped into slumber with the threat of the dream hanging over her. She imagined the way she would shimmy out the window beside her bed, a knife in her boot, another on her hip, and one clenched in her teeth to pick the lock of the gate. (Well, that part about picking the lock was squarely in her imagination, but she liked to dream.) The moonlight would streak the streets like spilled silver, and she'd creep away, leading Varlet, heading north again.

In the meantime, she familiarized herself with Yeglorn's streets with Cait by her side, an unknowing accomplice in her plan to flee.

Life spilled from every crevice of Yeglorn's twisting, cobblestoned streets. In a courtyard, children tossed a ball of stitched leather among themselves, catching and balancing it on their thighs just above the knee before passing it along. They giggled, the sound mingling with the clatter of hooves as a line of men on horseback galloped past Briand and Cait, their hats slung low over their eyes and their long coats dusty from the plains. Riders, Cait explained to Briand as they walked, did all sorts of work, from herding cattle and horses to delivering messages or hunting wolves or outlaws. It was the most common job for a young man in Estria besides rancher or breeder.

"It was always my dream to be a rider," Cait said as she paused below a stone arch leading to the markets. "But as I said, it's the most common job for a young man."

Cait reminded Briand a little of Reela, the young half-tyyrian Monarchist who'd been killed by Seekers when they'd fled her father's estate before destroying the Barrow Bridge. Thinking of Reela gave her a throb of pain in her chest that she'd been smothering under

189

work or sleep or planning for the future. Now, she pulled in a deep breath and allowed herself to feel it for a moment—just a moment. She had a bright, fierce energy to her, the lord's daughter did. She made up her mind with resolute determination, and she burned like a star. Briand felt like a shadow beside her, silent and dark, slipping away and coming back again, always behind. But she liked it, having someone else to wrench attentions away and command the gazes of the room. Cait was fearless and fearsome, the perfect ally in conversation and exploration.

Briand would miss her when she was gone.

"You're excellent with a horse," Briand protested. She knew little of Estrian customs, but these people seemed practical, if nothing else. Why should they care about what was between a rider's legs?

She said as much. Cait laughed, and it was a thin sound. "Estrians are a free people, but there are limits to their deviation from Austrisian propriety."

Cait liked to say things like that. Like she was Nath, quoting passages from a book.

"So they'll let you ride horses and get a little dirty, but..."

"But at the end of the day, I still have to be a lady," Cait finished. She made a face. "Meanwhile, Sobin would like nothing more than to design fashion in Tasglorn, but that's not exactly a wind-blessed choice for an Estrian lord's son either."

Estrians, Briand had noticed, were obsessed with the wind. They seemed to have dozens of sayings that related everything from love to money to the wind's ethereal and eternal motions. "An unrequited love is a cold wind on broken teeth." Or, "a quarrelsome friend is like sand in the wind." "Misfortune comes upon a man unbundled against it like a winter wind." "A smile is like a cool breeze to a laborer's back." And so forth. Perhaps she shouldn't be surprised, as they were enchanted with the sky in general. They seemed to believe, on a fundamental level, that Estria owned the sky, and the other provinces were only borrowing it. They owned their bits of sky proudly, with kites and flags, and Estria blessed them with lavish sunsets and that beautiful, encompassing wind that never ceased to ripple across the plains and through the streets of the city.

Cait led Briand into the market, stopping at the nearest stall to peruse a pile of yellow fruits shaped like long ovals with a strange fringe of bumps at the end.

"Feet fruit," Cait said to Briand, who had to agree that they did resemble knobby feet with too many toes at the ends.

She purchased two, and when Briand tried hers, it was shockingly sweet. Juice leaked down her chin as she took another bite. This was sunshine in food form.

Beyond the food stalls, pens and cages lined the road. Sheep, pigs, even a colt with spots on its face. Cait wandered, looking leisurely at the animals. A woman with a fluffy cat perched on her shoulders beckoned to them.

"Fancy a pet, loves? I've got exotics from every corner of the kingdom!"

"The sand cats would eat a bird if I brought it home," Cait murmured, her eyes on a fluttering white bird with blue tail feathers that trailed to the ground.

Briand laughed in agreement, and then a shiver went through her, accompanied by a flash of a thought—a warm fire, a delicious taste of meat in her mouth, a hand under her chin.

She stopped, chills rushing down her back. The thought had not been hers. Something rustled in the cage to her left. Briand stepped closer.

"Briand?" Cait turned back to look for her.

Inside the cage, a dark shape lay curled in a ball. A tongue flicked from a pointed head. Briand felt another shiver of apprehension.

It was communicating with her like a dragon.

She again had the impulse of a warm fire and food in her mouth and belly. She reached for the cage as soon as the woman's back was turned, lifting the fabric.

A faint wheeze came from the shadow beneath.

"What about this one?" she asked the woman, her calm tone belying her pounding heart.

The merchant snatched off her shoulder-scarf and tossed it over the cage. "That is nothing. Just a rock lizard. It is not for sale."

Briand opened her mouth to counter, but something caught her eye that made her stomach twist. A hooded figure dressed in black, moving through the market with the grace of a snake. He didn't appear to see her as she stepped back into the shadow of the stall. He paused to regard a fluttering piece of paper nailed to the whipping platform before he moved on, leaving the paper to twist and curl in the breeze. She squinted. REWARD, it read. She couldn't make out the rest without moving closer.

Then the figure was gone, and she could breathe again.

"Are you all right?" Cait asked.

She nodded wordlessly.

The cage rustled, drawing Briand's attention again. Another image filled her mind, and Briand almost dropped the cloth as she saw Drune's face in her mind, and felt another flood of something that felt like recognition.

"Sieya?"

TWENTY-FIVE

BRIAND HADN'T BEEN able to discover how Sieya had fallen into the keeping of the woman selling the exotic animals, as the woman refused to talk about it after she'd been convinced to sell the dracule for all the coins Cait had in her pockets, but the dracule appeared to be none the worse for wear except for a ravenous appetite for sweets. She had grown larger, her tail longer and her back ridged with spines, her curved teeth longer and sharper. Briand released the dracule in her room, and watched as the creature nibbled at shoes, touched her nose to the furniture, and then romped to the window like an overgrown puppy to peer through the glass at the courtyard below. Her breath fogged the pane, and she made a growling sound in her throat before flicking her tongue against it experimentally.

"Sieya," Briand called.

Did the dracule remember the name?

The dracule looked at her, and an image of a sweetmeat filled Briand's mind with a tinge of hopefulness. It was a question.

Kael had suggested she use this opportunity to hone her skills. He'd barely shown a flicker of emotion at the revelation that Sieya was alive and back in their company. He'd been stalking about the manor in a black mood. Maybe the reminder of Drune was what had him so irritable and tense.

Briand was tense too—the addition of the dracule complicated things. It would be impossible to take Sieya, and she already felt the ache of leaving the dracule behind.

She focused on the immediate. "You want a treat?" she said, interpreting the thought from the dracule.

The dracule's ears pricked forward at the word *treat*.

"Well, come on, then."

The cook staff took one look at Sieya and flattened themselves against the walls. The head cook shrieked when he turned around and caught a glimpse of the massive reptilian creature on the ground before him.

"What is it?" he shouted, brandishing a ladle like a sword.

"A dracule," Briand said. "Don't worry, she is tame."

They all looked at her with a mixture of horror and fear.

"Oh!" Briand heard behind her. She turned and saw Cait, hands over her mouth. "It's bigger than I realized."

Sieya trotted over to Cait and sniffed the edge of her boots. She sneezed sparks, and one ignited a bit of discarded paper on the floor in a tiny tumbleweed of flame that Briand stamped out.

"The cats are going to hate this," Cait said.

The cats did, indeed, hate Sieya's presence. They spit and hissed at the sight of the dracule, fluffing their fur and lashing their tails.

On the other hand, Tibus was more delighted to see the little creature, and even Nath cracked a smile at the sight of her trying to wiggle her way into a box.

In fact, large domesticated sand cats aside, the whole household was soon charmed by the dracule and her aggressive desire for sweets, which she begged, charmed, or stole from anyone foolish enough to eat in her presence. She had learned to sit on her haunches and stretch out her neck, mouth wide open, tongue uncurled like a flag hanging off a rampart. Sometimes she wheedled a little song in the back of her throat, a mournful whine accompanied by a longing stare at whatever morsel was currently being denied her. Briand had no idea how the dracule wasn't the size of a horse already, given her eating habits.

Having Sieya there made the plan to leave more difficult. The little creature was always following her, tail lashing as she was distracted by a bird or a mouse, ears pricking up at distant voices or the clatter of hooves outside the courtyard gate. She scratched at closed doors and complained in a growling moan when she was detained anywhere for too long. Once, when Briand experimentally shut her in a closet, Sieya wailed so loudly that both the cats came running with ears flattened to hiss at the door on the other side. The images that flooded from the dracule's mind to Briand's were catastrophic—waters rising, thunderstorms, infernos devouring whole forests. As soon as she was released, however, she was circling Briand's heels, sniffing her ankles and projecting thoughts of tasty morsels.

"You," Briand said, feeling a touch irritated, "are overly dramatic."

Sieya sneezed innocently and thought about treats. She planted her hindquarters on the tiled floor and fixed her eyes on Briand with great expectation.

"No," Briand said, pointing a finger in an ineffectual gesture of disapproval.

From the tenor of the dracule's thoughts, scoldings had little to no effect.

"Can you reach into her mind as before?" Kael inquired when he and Briand crossed paths in the hall after dinner. Something glimmered in his eyes, and she looked away, her heart a traitor against her.

"Easily," she said, careful to keep her voice steady and indifferent. "She communicates with me as readily as I do with her."

"Do you believe she's been trained?"

"Well, someone's been spoiling her." She paused. "I don't think she's had any sort of run-ins with anyone like me, if that's what you mean. The mind-talking seems to come... naturally. Drune mentioned a sort of memory pool that dragons draw upon."

A shadow passed over Kael's eyes at the mention of Drune's name.

"Keep practicing," he said. "The more you learn, the more you'll be prepared for the caverns."

The thought of the mission she was leaving made her uneasy, but she didn't have a choice.

She would be gone before the week was up.

TWENTY-SIX

BRIAND WOKE TO the sound of horse hooves and the groan of the gate. Someone was arriving. Her head throbbed with the memory of dreams about arguments with Kael and interrogations with Seekers. The taste of dread lay in her bones as she rose and went to the window to see who had come.

A black coach with gold filigree on the wheels and around the door stood in the yard. The master and mistress of the house, along with Kael and Tibus, waited beside it as the coachman stepped down to open the door. Kael stood with his hands clasped behind his back and his face as somber as always, but for some reason, one Briand couldn't quite decipher, she knew he was pleased.

As she watched, a woman stepped out. Her boots crunched on the gravel of the yard, and the master of the house hurried forward to take her hand.

"Welcome," Briand heard him say, his voice floating up to her window.

The woman inclined her head. The brim of the top hat she wore shaded her face, but Briand could see a pair of wine-colored lips, full and smiling the smile of one who knows slightly more than everyone else around her and who also knows exactly how to play that to her advantage. She wore a dress of black and white stripes, a corset that nipped her narrow waist, and a low-slung utility belt over it with a scabbard that rested on her hip. Her hands were gloved, and for a moment Briand felt a skitter of panic, thinking of Seekers, but then she saw the gloves were fingerless, and made of lace. Ladies' fare. Not the thick, gray gloves that encased the magic hands of the Sighted.

Kael offered the woman his arm, and she curled her hand around his elbow like it belonged to her.

~

The woman's name was Maera. Her skin was caramel brown, her hair a luxurious black. She had a way of looking at people and making them feel as though they were the most brilliant speaker in the room, or the stupidest. She could make even Lord Barria stutter with a flick of her groomed eyebrow, and she had Tibus blushing after one flutter of her lashes.

Briand immediately found herself fascinated.

"Dragonsayer," Maera said when they were introduced, and the edges of her mouth curled in a pensive smile. "I've heard much about you from Kael."

Briand was startled at that. A glance at Kael told her nothing, as he was as impassive as always. But Maera dimpled as if she had a secret.

"Maera is Tasnian," Tibus explained later, after dinner when Maera, Kael, and Lord Barria were sequestered away in private and the rest of them sat in one of the courtyards, sipping from an after-dinner wine and listening to the wind chimes that hung from the trees. "She's from the capital city, like Kael. It's why they're both so watchful and suspicious of everyone.

Tibus, like all good Austrisians who did not hail from Tasna, didn't trust those that did. Except his beloved leader. But he had choice words even for Kael that evening. He'd had a little too much wine at dinner and was drinking more now, and his tongue was loose. Briand leaned closer, encouraging him with a nod. She wanted to hear more about Kael's past. It might grant her more understanding of the man.

"They watch everything like they're waiting to pounce on the wrong word," he murmured, tipping his head back to gaze at the sky. He chuckled liquidly.

"Inscrutable," Briand offered. It had been one of her uncle's favorite words.

"Exactly. Not to speak ill of Kael, mind you. His manner serves him well."

"How long have you known Kael?" Tibus had served her uncle for years. She didn't know their original connection, although it was undeniably strong.

"More than a decade," Tibus said. "I trained in Tasna as a mercenary, and it was there that we met." He smiled at some private thought. "I was younger then, and confident. Kael challenged me to a swordfight, and like the cocky bloke that I was, I vowed to knock him on his back. I was disarmed in ten blows."

She leaned forward, fascinated and amused. "Did you often duel noblemen's sons?"

Tibus snorted. "Of course not. But I didn't know who he was. He was wearing plain clothing, fooling us all. But then, he's never liked to claim his rank when he can escape it. Half the Monarchists don't even know whose son he is."

"Is his father a Monarchist?"

Tibus looked troubled at the mention of Kael's father. "He is," he said, taking another swallow. "Of a kind."

"Of a kind?" She didn't understand.

Tibus wiped his mouth with his sleeve. He started to respond, but then he looked past her and his eyes widened a fraction. "I shouldn't say such things. The wine has made me careless."

She turned her head. Kael stood behind them. There was no telling what he'd heard.

But Kael only said, "We're gathering in Lord Barria's lower study to discuss the mission."

Briand stood and followed Tibus inside to Lord Barria's lower study, which was a fine, paneled room with stuffed wolf heads on the walls and a long, petrified bone of some ancient monster mounted behind the desk. Maera sat in one of the chairs, slender fingers curved over the ends of the armrests, her head tipped slightly to one side, her mouth curved in an almost-smile. Beside her, Lord Barria stood with his hand resting on a map spread across the desk. His fingers were splayed across Estria, and beneath his thumb was Sythra, the southern province, the curve of it like an elephant's head. At the lower part, someone had written CAVERNS across a stretch of marks for mountains, and then, underneath that, DRAGONS.

Briand took her place between Tibus and Nath. She could feel Maera watching her, curiously this time. It did not feel like an unfriendly gaze.

"Now that Maera is here," Kael said to them all, "we'll leave for Sythra at first light. Our story is simple—we're attendants escorting the Lady Barria to meet her potential suitor."

She had to leave tonight, then. She felt a clench of panic.

"We'll travel by horseback to the coastal city of Jaseel, where we'll assume our disguises and rent a coach." Kael signaled to Nath, who spread a second map across the table. A diagram of an estate.

"This was drawn by memory from a former servant of Kul's, so it might be incomplete, but it's the best we've got," Nath said. He pointed to several places on the map, naming things as he did so. "There are the outer walls, the moat, and the poisonous garden and stone maze. Kul used Cahan's palace grounds as his inspiration. The caverns are, according to the accounts we could find in treasure hunter lore, beneath the water gardens." He paused. "The only problem is that the water is full of shivsharks, imported from the jungles of Bhan."

"Of course it is," Tibus muttered. "And how are we planning to keep our skin on our bones?"

"We have a plan for that," Nath said.

"Tibus, Nath, and I will take the role of guards," Kael said. "Briand, a lady's handmaid."

Kael began to lay out more specific plans for when they arrived at the estate. As Briand listened, doubts kept tugging at her mind like fishhooks. What would become of the mission when she left?

She owed them no loyalty. She'd tried to drum it into her head a thousand times by now. She was merely a tool to be used, like a bit in a horse's mouth, the blade of a knife, the sole of a boot.

But another part of her, the foolish, loyal part, looked at their faces half bathed in shadow as they gazed at the map of the estate and made their plans, and it whispered that if she left now, what would they do? Would they find a way to get the treasure anyway? If there were dragons, like the myths said, would they be consumed?

Her eyes returned to Kael as if drawn by a cord.

No, she had to look out for herself. She was the only one who was going to do it. She didn't even know there was a treasure, let alone dragons guarding it. She consoled herself with that.

But still, she worried.

Maera watched her across the table, her eyes thoughtful. Briand snapped her attention to the map as Nath explained how they were going to gain entrance to the caves, and her heart drummed a rhythm of dread against her ribs.

~

The rain was still falling when Briand went in search of Sieya after supper. The dracule wasn't in any of her usual haunts—the kitchen, the pantry, or lying in front of the cellar door in hopes someone would descend into the depths of what amounted to a food dungeon—and so she was combing the rooms one by one.

She felt a tingle of the creature's thoughts and followed it like a trail of crumbs to the library. She stepped inside and felt for the wall. The room was swathed in shadow, the only light coming from the windows as lightning flashed.

When it did, it illuminated Kael's face.

He sat in a chair, elbows braced on his knees, his face carved from stone. He held the satchel in his hand, her packet, with the maps carefully marked in her careful, crude handwriting in the other.

She stopped dead.

"Planning an extra excursion?" he said. His tone was light, laced with anger.

Sieya crept from beneath the chair, tail curling around Kael's feet. She breathed a spurt of sparks in her direction. Kael didn't look down. Orange light danced along his jaw for an eye blink and was gone with the breath.

"When were you planning on leaving?"

Briand held still despite the alarm coursing through her. No reason to deny it, not now. "Soon."

She couldn't explain. He wouldn't hear it. He would only hear betrayal. There were too many secrets.

He leaned forward. Tension licked along his cheekbones along with the shifting shadows. His eyes were pools of black. He was angry, really angry. It hit her like a slap.

"Did you really think I'd let you go? Did you think you'd really be able to simply slip away?"

"I thought I wasn't your prisoner," Briand said to buy time. Sieya was whining in her mind, sending visions of treats. She kept her focus on Kael even as she checked the room at the edges of her vision. They were alone. The window behind him was shut and bolted. Rain slung against the glass.

"I serve the prince. The prince needs you. I'm bound to my orders." He said it flatly. Heavily. But she was startled to see betrayal flash in his eyes.

"I know," she said, and for once, she did. "I understand your position. You have to understand my position, too."

Perhaps those words would be enough to convince him that she left only because she was the scrappy, thoughtless guttersnipe who always left, just as he said before.

She took a step back.

He was on his feet before she could blink, closing the gap between them in two strides. He pinned her to the wall beside the door, his hands enclosing her wrists, lightly but with enough force to hold her in place.

"I'm sorry," he said. His eyebrows lifted a little as he said the words. "I do understand, but I can't let you go."

"I'm sorry, too," she said. And she was. So sorry. She ached with it.

She stood on her tiptoes and pressed her lips to his. One kiss. She allowed herself that because, if she did this right, she would never see him again.

She felt the shock ripple through him as he pulled back and stared down at her. She stared back, holding him with her gaze. Trying to give him one glimpse of her head and her heart in that look. See me, she begged silently. For once.

And then she knifed him.

TWENTY-SEVEN

NATH'S MOUNT WOULDN'T stand still as he tried to dismount when they made camp. The fool horse kept shying sideways, snorting, as if something were hiding in the bushes. He had no patience for stupid creatures, not now. Not with the guttersnipe on the run, and everything in confusion, and Kael as tense and furious and blisteringly calm as he'd ever seen him all at once. Nath dropped to the ground, spitting curses at the animal, and kicked the underbrush until a snake slithered away toward the campfire. The horse reared back, snorting, and Nath drew his knife, but the snake was already dead, its head impaled with a quivering blade. Nath raised his head and saw their leader standing by the unlit fire, looking at the snake and his blade buried in its skull as if some sort of clue to where the dragonsayer had fled was written in the way its skin was sliced.

"Sir," Tibus said from behind them, and Kael seemed to come back to himself. He stepped forward and yanked the knife from the snake before kicking the body away into the grass.

"Yes, Tibus?"

"There's been a report. A possible sighting."

Kael turned to hear it, and Nath struggled to tether and unsaddle his still-snorting mount. He could hear Tibus speaking quietly, something about Cahan's soldiers and the latest sighting of the Seekers. The magical bastards were moving north, the same direction as Briand, and it was uncertain whether they were aware of Kael's group. The Seekers could be toying with them, or hoping to follow them. He undid the straps and yanked the saddle off the horse with too much force.

She could have trusted him. She could have stayed. She didn't have to be such a... such a guttersnipe.

And now she was out there. Alone once again. Vulnerable as a baby kitten in the face of those Hunters. Running away from who knows what. The mission? Herself?

He swung around, the saddle in his arms, and caught sight of Kael's face in an unguarded moment. Their leader looked as stricken as Nath felt, but then, as Nath watched, he folded the emotion away behind his eyes. Nath wanted to swear again, but this time not at the snake.

"What have you done to us?" he said helplessly, thinking of her, with her angles and freckles and wild, fierce energy.

The woman spy, Maera, sat on a log by the unlit fire. She drew a long-stemmed pipe from the pouch at her waist, lit it, and stuck it between her teeth.

She'd insisted on coming along, and none of the rest of them had had the presence of mind to refuse her in the confusion. Kael had been bleeding and throwing things around as he grabbed supplies; Cait had been weeping; and Tibus had been trying to milk information from Kael while Nath cut away his shirt to assess the knife wound while thunder clanged overhead, drowning out their voices.

In the end, Maera was the one who'd sewn Kael up and given him a stiff drink to accompany it. She was the one who'd said something sternly to him, in a low voice no one else could hear above the roar of the rain on the roof, and then he'd gathered himself and headed for the stables. It was the sort of thing Nath usually did, when he wasn't a maelstrom inside. But the guttersnipe running away had gutted him, making him almost useless.

Maera was all the things about Kael that Nath couldn't stand, and none of the things that he loved about the leader, except perhaps clever. Too clever.

She closed her lips around the pipe and inhaled. Watching them. Seeing his distress.

He dropped the saddle over a fallen tree and grabbed a bucket before heading for the stream to clear his head.

~

Kael lit a fire. With his gift of magic, the wet wood exploded into a blaze almost immediately. Bits of flame shot up to the sky in a plume of sparks and ash. He sat back, folding his hands under his chin, grinding his teeth together. A headache clamped around the base of his skull.

She was gone. Vanished like a spark into the night. Couldn't she just, for once, do something that surprised him and stay?

But she had surprised him. That kiss.

He could barely see straight, he was so furious. His arm ached where she'd knifed him, just a flesh wound to distract him so he'd let her go, and Maera had stitched it because Nath was almost beside himself. His whole body trembled from exhaustion—he'd been training all day, and awake half the night before deciphering a coded message from Jehn, and now he was on his feet in the middle of a rainstorm with a stab wound and a suffocating fear that the guttersnipe had already been snatched by Seekers, or drowned in a river, or eaten by wolves.

She was gone on the eve of the mission, with Seekers practically breathing at their heels. She was madness incarnate to run away at a time like this.

Maera sat opposite him, smoking that damned pipe. She only did it because people hated it. She and Catfoot would be best friends. They were both so infuriating.

"You're worried," Maera said. "It's showing."

She was right. His control over his voice, his expression, had grown thin. He let his breath out slowly, regathering himself. He was not a man given to rage. He was the master of his temper.

He was shaking.

"I'm a good tracker," she said. "I'll find your dragonsayer. She's unlikely to be dead yet. The Seekers are keeping pace with us."

"She's alive," he said, more to himself than to her. Maera was many things, but comforting was never one of them.

Maera raised one eyebrow. "Ah," she said. She fixed her gaze on him and put the pipe back in her mouth.

She was as close as a sister to him. And he was going to throttle her if she didn't stop that staring.

"I'll find her," Maera said again, and this time she was reassuring him more gently.

He'd fumed for ten minutes before he realized he wasn't even thinking about the mission or how they were doomed.

Just that damned Catfoot and how terrified he was that they wouldn't find her again.

TWENTY-EIGHT

AUBERON RODE BESIDE the Hunter. The land around them was a sea of golden grass studded with flowers, like a scene from a tapestry. But he barely saw it. He hated the wide open sky of Estria almost as much as he hated riding a horse. He'd been born and bred for the city and its comforts, not this nomadic drudgery of riding, camping, and riding again.

When he found that girl, he was going to make her sorry for every single blister he'd gotten pursuing her.

He needed to sleep. He'd find her in his dreams. The edges of her awareness had begun to bleed into them while she slept, giving him clues to where he could find her. She was currently moving north, judging by the sounds of the wildlife.

"We'll make camp," he said.

The Hunter nodded. They couldn't speak; they had no tongues. He found it disgusting, but then, he'd never understood anything about their devotion to their calling.

He dismounted, eager to be done with this.

~

Rain drummed against the windowpanes of the inn as Briand sat on the edge of the bed, her belongings spread out on the coverlet. She sorted through the coins she had left with one hand and chewed her lower lip as she counted.

There wasn't much.

She'd earned most of the coins playing Dubbok in seedy taverns with dirty cards and dirtier patrons willing to bet that a skinny waif-girl like her would lose. She didn't even have the energy to savor their shock at being wrong. She was too busy disappearing after gathering her earnings. She had too many targets on her back as it was, and she had to keep moving. She didn't have a set destination, although she found herself heading toward Kyreia, like a carrier pigeon set free. She wanted to see the ruin of her father's house. She wanted to look on the wreckage and know it was true, that her roots were truly turned to ash.

A board creaked outside her door. Briand lifted her head, her senses straining. The innkeeper? He'd leered openly at her, a young female traveling unaccompanied, as though that made her his for the taking. He'd stood too close when he'd unlocked the door to her room, and when she'd given him a look to communicate that he needed to step away, he grinned and picked something from his teeth.

Charming.

She wanted to smash those teeth in.

She scooped the coins into their bag, tucked it back into her shirt, and picked up her knife. She rolled off the bed, careful to land cat feet-quiet, and crept to the door to listen. Another creak sounded outside, like someone shifting their weight on old boards. She took a step back, and collided with solid flesh.

She kicked over the lamp burning on the table beside the door, plunging the room into darkness, and then she was ducking under the arm that grabbed at her, heading for the window that was just a gray square in the blackness. She heard a thud behind her, and a whispered curse, and then she was at the window, on the sill and poised to jump.

The ground two stories below taunted her. She'd chosen the height to keep out intruders. The building across the alley was too far to jump, also why she'd chosen this room. But there was a vine clinging to the wall, and she might be light enough for it to hold her weight.

A hand grabbed her arm.

"I know cats have nine lives," he breathed in her ear. "But you have already spent so many, Catfoot."

"Kael," she said.

He'd found her. Despite all her precautions, her extra care and her tricks, he'd found her.

The door slammed against the wall as Tibus stumbled inside. He'd been the one in the hall, not the innkeeper. "Sir," he said to Kael, breathing hard as a bull. "Seekers. They're in the inn. They're coming up the stairs as I speak."

Dimly from the floor below, Briand heard the sound of breaking glass, and a clang of something heavy being thrown.

Somehow, Auberon had found her.

Kael dragged her back from the window. A fine sheen of sweat on his brow made his skin gleam in the light from the hall. "Briand—"

"I'm not coming with you. I can't."

He didn't move. "You can't keep running on your own. You won't survive being hunted like this."

"I'm not your prince's puppet!"

The lines in his face didn't soften, but his eyes held hers, and she was seen to her core. "I know," he said. And then, "You left."

"You don't know what I've done," she said. "You don't know—"

"At this moment, I don't care."

She opened her mouth to convince him, but then he was kissing her, his fingers grazing her chin and jaw. When he drew back, he breathed, "You left, and it made me so afraid. Please don't do that again."

She was speechless. Her mind was spinning. Was this a dream too, just like the ones with Auberon? She touched his mouth.

"We've got to go," Tibus warned from the doorway.

"We're stronger together than apart," Kael said. His voice was raw, low. His fingertips were still on her jaw. His eyes burned a frantic light. "I can't fight you and run from them. Not at the same time. Please."

Somehow, she found herself putting her hand into his.

TWENTY-NINE

HER HAND WAS in his, and Kael was breathing again after days of no air. The memory of the kiss was like a burn. He was still gripping the dragonsayer's hand as Tibus disappeared into the corridor again, and he pulled her after him toward the window she'd just been considering leaping from like the Catfoot she was.

If they couldn't go down, they'd go up.

She was ahead of him when they reached the window, pulling *him,* turning her head to look up. She knew what he was thinking. He felt a rush of sudden admiration as she pointed to the vines.

"They're the same ones from the forest when we were on the run together. They'll hold our weight." She looked at him, squinting against the rain. "Lift me up."

He put his hands on her waist and hoisted her, and she grasped the vines and scrambled up the rest of the way to the roof. He was right behind her, and below he heard the crash of boots and a shout. Then they were sliding across the slick tiles toward the far edge of the inn, and lightning lit the outline of the dragonsayer ahead of him. She paused, gathering herself before making the leap. He was right behind her. They landed on the next roof, slipping in the rain, and then they were running to where the forest beckoned at the end of the row of houses.

The dragonsayer tumbled to the ground ahead of him and was already on her feet when he landed beside her. She ducked beneath the branches, and he kept pace with her. She wasn't going to disappear again, not now that he'd found her.

They ran and ran until the rain had abated to a thick mist. Two rocks came together to make a hollow dry place, and they stopped to wait for Tibus in the previously agreed-upon spot.

The dragonsayer sat with her back to the stone, her legs pulled up against her chest. The silence filled up with the sound of rain returning, a patterning of droplets on the leaves. This was familiar. The waiting, the rain, the quiet wrapping them up.

She was watching him. He turned his head and caught her, and she didn't look away. She was glistening from the rain. She was all arms and cheekbones and questions in her eyes he couldn't answer, because he didn't know.

He hesitated, then sank down beside her, close enough to touch.

She couldn't know it, but she made him want to talk. She made him want to shed his cool exterior like an old shirt and pour himself out in stories. Something about her made him want to lecture, to cajole, to explain, to jest even. She dragged stories of his childhood from him with her skittish smile and curious eyes. She made him ache to make himself known to her.

"You make me want to trust you," he said. He leaned closer.

Her mouth curved up ruefully. "Don't sound so resentful about it."

She curled her fingers into his hair and leaned into him. She was rough skin and the scent of rain. He never wanted to let her go.

"Why did you do it?" he asked, bold with her against him. "Why did you run?"

She hesitated. "I have been seeing the Seeker in my dreams."

"What?" He pulled back.

"Auberon. When we were captured, somehow he and I became linked. He was trying to use the link to find our location."

Kael was speechless. She'd run to protect them.

Tibus arrived before he could say anything else.

~

Tibus's hair was plastered to his forehead, and droplets streamed down his face and made rivulets on his shirt. Blood stained his sleeve, and he grimaced as he moved his arm to wipe the water from his eyes.

"Is she with you?" he whispered to Kael, and then Briand shifted and stood, moving into his field of vision, and Tibus lumbered forward and grabbed her in a hug. She tightened her arms around him for a second as tears sprang to her eyes, mostly from the rush of fear she'd just had as they'd fled, and the sting of the rain.

After a moment, Tibus drew back. He clapped her on the shoulder again, as if reassuring himself again that she was really there.

"You gave us a fright," he said gruffly over the pouring rain. "We had you again, safe with us, and then you were gone. Don't let them act otherwise. They were worried. Kael almost tore the countryside apart looking—"

"Seekers are hot on our tail," Kael said. He was calm, collected Kael again, the one that resisted scrutiny, the persona snapped over him like a curtain closed across a window.

But he'd kissed her. He'd kissed her like she'd kissed him, even though she'd followed hers with a knife to the arm. Even though hers had been a distraction. Was that why he'd done it? To distract her, like she'd distracted him?

"We ought to keep moving," Kael said. "We can make the morning ferry if we press on through this storm."

"Wait," Briand said.

He looked at her. His gaze, as always, pierced her, but there was a softness to it now.

"I can always run again," she reminded him. "Perhaps I should."

"We will keep you safe," Kael said. "We need you. It's worth the risk. And I can teach you to resist with your mind—"

"I want your word that I can go free after this mission. That I'm a partner, not a prisoner. Not a pawn to be used over and over in these war games."

Like a game of Dubbok, when she had the right cards in her hand. It was the same, the way the future hardened into something tangible and assured, and she knew she was going to win if she could hold herself together long enough to play them right.

Kael was listening.

She continued, speaking in a measured tone even though the words begged to spill out in a plea. She was not going to beg. She was vulnerable enough right now as it was.

"I want your word that I won't be in chains, and you won't ask about the Hermit. You won't make insinuations. You'll trust me. You'll treat me as an equal. And when it's finished, I can walk away."

Tibus shifted, looking over his shoulder at the way he'd come as if trying to grant them privacy. But Kael kept his attention focused on her. He'd blinked at the word *if* as though she'd shocked him by suggesting the possibility.

"We should go, sir," Tibus said. He was apologetic.

Briand stood her ground. "Well?"

She was ready to run. They'd lose her in this rain. But she didn't want to. Her heart slammed against her chest, and she couldn't breathe as she realized she wanted him to say yes more than anything.

Kael hesitated. She knew he was thinking it over, weighing the costs. Then he nodded.

"I swear it," he said.

THIRTY

TRUE TO HIS word, Kael didn't bind her like a captured prisoner, and true to her word, Briand didn't try to run. They moved carefully around each other, as if each were waiting for the other to act. Briand felt skittish as a colt. Kael watched her often. But whenever she turned her head and intercepted his gaze, he looked away.

They crossed the river when the rain had let up enough to show the dawn, pink and shivering at the edge of the horizon. A cluster of wooden buildings pretending to be a town squatted on a spit of sand and marsh on the opposite bank. Briand didn't know where they were. The upper part of Estria, at least. She'd been moving from place to place without marking carefully.

They found Maera and Nath waiting at the inn. From across the room she could see that Nath was a pillar of anxiety, held together by pure resolve, his hair mussed from anxious tugging and his chin grizzled with several days' worth of growth. He hunched over the table, arms crossed over his chest. Maera lounged beside him with her long legs stretched out on the chair in front of her, her hair a swirling wave of ink over her shoulder. She wore a red cloak that draped around her shoulders and puddled on the floor, a pair of elbow-length leather gloves, and bronze airship pilot's goggles pushed into her curls. Her lips were a stamp of ruby against her

221

olive skin. She was turning heads, and she met the stares with the faintest of smiles, each flick of her lips like the curl of a beckoning finger.

When they entered, Nath spotted them first. He took a huge swig of the drink in front of him, finishing the whole thing in a gulp. He wiped his mouth and gave Briand a shaky scowl as he stood.

"Guttersnipe," he said. "That was a devil of a thing to do. We thought... I feared that..." He sighed. "Just don't do it again."

"Tibus already gave me that speech," she replied, her throat thick with emotion.

"He probably butchered it," Nath said with a shaky laugh. He pushed out a chair for her, and she sat. Tibus and Kael took the places beside her, and a server appeared with drinks and hot food.

Maera didn't speak at first. Her dark eyes studied Briand, then the others in turn. Her red lips pulled down in a frown.

"You're late," she said to Kael, leaning forward. A question, not an accusation.

"Seekers," he responded.

The word was like a breath of ice across the table, sending shards of fear into everyone.

Nath's hand hesitated where he was reaching for a stick of bread. The color drained from his face, and he sat back quickly, his hand going to the weapon at his hip as if by instinct.

"I lost 'em in the forest," Tibus explained. "They didn't pursue me very hard, since Briand was with Kael and she's the one they want. We're ahead of

222

them now, if they're coming this way at all. Might have shaken them off."

"We'll head south before nightfall," Kael said. "Horseback until we reach the city, as planned. We'll stay ahead of them, Nath."

Nath gave a tight nod.

"What about her?" Maera asked, gesturing at Briand with a flick of her gloved hand. "Is she going to run again?"

Everyone looked at Briand.

She appreciated Maera's bluntness, Briand decided. It was refreshing to have someone speaking so plainly, rather than the cryptic riddles she'd grown accustomed to with this lot.

"Kael and I have come to an agreement," she said. "I'm not going to run. I'm not a prisoner, either."

"Good," Maera grunted, satisfied with that explanation. She pushed her chair back and stood in a swirl of red cloak. "That's settled. Let's get out of here. I need the wind in my face again."

~

The horses they'd procured had a little mare among them with a stripe in her forelock, and the sight of it made Briand miss Varlet with a stab of pain in her chest. Varlet, Sieya, Sobin, Cait... She sucked in a breath to calm the spasm of feeling, but it didn't work. She was becoming far too attached. If only she could deaden her heart. Every throb of it seemed to work against her.

"What happened to Sieya?" she asked Kael when she trusted her voice to be steady and disaffected.

He kept his eyes on the horizon as he answered. He'd been cool toward her since Tibus had joined them, even more so now that they were in the company of the others. "The dracule is still with Lord Barria and his family. Much to the chagrin of their cats, I imagine."

A bubble of surprised laughter lodged in Briand's throat. "I didn't know you'd noticed their little feud. And Varlet?"

"The mare is also still in Lord Barria's care."

She breathed out in relief.

"Cait? Sobin? How are they?"

"Anxious about you, no doubt."

She could imagine Cait pacing in her distress, exclaiming angrily, Sobin sitting with a perplexed look, as if he could make things right if he just sorted everything out in his head and understood it.

How she missed them.

"Tell me more about these dreams," Kael said in a low voice, and she recounted them to him. He listened, his expression grim, as she told of the shrinking cell and Auberon's threats and deductions. Then he explained to her what he did to keep the Seekers from his mind. The falling rain made a curtain around them, and she leaned close to catch his words.

The rain faded into cloudy, restless skies as the company of Monarchists and dragonsayer traveled south, and the landscape changed from trees and rivers to rocks and gullies swollen from the recent downpours. Brown water streamed through little canyons, and mud sucked at the hooves of the horses.

They made camp in the wilderness when the sky turned red. Nath fixed a simple supper of jerky and biscuits and tea, and they laid out their bedrolls for sleep. Kael took the first watch, and Maera joined him at the edge of the camp, her shape a soft shadow beside his. The quiet murmur of their voices made Briand drowsy despite her internal state of vigilance.

Nath slept on her left, and Kael had laid out his bed on her right. She'd given him a bald stare when he'd arranged it so, and the Monarchist had only lifted one eyebrow in that way of his, the impenetrable aura he projected that made her feel as if she were over-reading the situation.

Some time after everyone else had retired to their bedrolls, Kael returned to his, leaving Maera with the watch alone. He settled beside Briand and stretched out on his back with one arm slung up over his head and the other resting by his side, near his knife. She wasn't sure if he was keeping ready to grab it in case of an attacker, or guarding it from her.

Briand lay awake in the darkness despite her weariness, fearing sleep and dreams. Thoughts ran up and down the corridors of her mind, hand in hand with emotions she would rather banish. Everything was in a confusion. She thought she was angry, because she felt on fire with feeling, but perhaps it was something else. Every time Kael moved beside her, she felt it to her bones. In the darkness, she was joined to him with a thousand threads of attention that kept her awake until she could no longer stave off exhaustion.

The dream came suddenly. She was in the cell, the bars too close again, and Auberon standing close to them, fury marring his features. "You were right there. I found you."

She let him rage as she stood and drew in a breath. She remembered what Kael had told her, and gathered herself. She could do this. She was strong. She was the dragonsayer. She could resist Seeker magic.

She focused on the bars. Move, she thought. Expand. The cell bars wavered and shivered but didn't budge.

Auberon staggered. "What are you doing?"

"Banishing you."

"He stepped forward and thrust his arm through the bars. He could reach her now.

She shut her eyes.

His hand was cold against her forehead as he clamped his fingers over her face. She could feel him trying to get at her mind. The thoughts sifted like restless leaves in a wind.

Not rage, Kael had told her. It isn't strong enough. It isn't deep enough. You must draw on deeper emotions. Loyalty.

She thought of Nath and Tibus. Reela. Cait and Sobin.

Hope.

She saw Estria at dawn, the grass rippling in a fresh wind, horses strung across the hills with their noses buried in wildflowers.

Love.

She saw her cousin. Her parents. The silly little dracule spitting sparks at her as it begged for a treat. Kael.

Pain lanced her abdomen. She was heaving. Auberon made a sound of pain and disbelief, and his hand was wrenched away. A wind rushed around her head.

"Briand."

She woke to see Kael leaning over her, his head outlined by stars above.

The memory of the pain lingered. She blinked.

"Are you all right?" he said quietly. His voice was gruff with sleep, and it made her stomach curl. She nodded and let her head fall back on the bedroll.

"It was the dream."

"And?"

"I... I did what you said."

Kael moved back, but she turned her hand and caught his fingers in a wordless question. She needed someone to hold on to. Just for tonight.

He didn't say anything, but his hand stayed against hers, and she fell asleep again, this time without dreams.

THIRTY-ONE

THE NEXT SEVERAL days were a grueling ride south, through increasingly dry landscape, occasionally sliced through by green rivers or a swath of scrubby vegetation. Nath, ever the tutor, explained to Briand that the upper half of Sythra was a desert, while the lower lands had a temperate climate that had led to the construction of many luxurious secondary estates by Tasnian lords.

"Our destination is one such estate," he continued. "Once occupied only a few months of the year, which gave treasure hunters time to try to enter. Now, though, according to our spies, the Butcher of Tasglorn spends most of his time there. Apparently, he was recently injured, and the hot Sythran climate is better for his health."

The journey grew more grim as they passed by towns and villages with burned houses, scorched fields, gaunt children.

"I don't understand," Briand said. "It looks like a war zone. Did the conflict between the Monarchists and Cahan do this?"

"It's merely the cost of Cahan's massive standing army," Nath replied crisply. "They pillage. They need food, and they'll take it from their own people."

"No," Kael said. It was the first thing he'd said in a while. "These towns showed resistance. They were loyal to Jehn, so Cahan's troops made an example of them."

Maera seemed to tighten all over at the sights they encountered, her lips thinning and her eyes slitting as if remembering something unbearable. She pulled up the hood of her cloak to shield her face before they rode through each of the towns. At one point, Kael directed his horse beside hers as if to further obscure her from any eyes that might turn her way. Briand wondered what history the spy had in these towns. What stories did she know about the scars this land, these people bore?

She hadn't dreamed of Auberon since she'd used what Kael had taught her. But she was fearful every time she closed her eyes in sleep, and she slept restlessly and woke with foreboding still lingering in her bones. It wasn't over, she knew that much.

When they stopped for camp in the evenings, Briand released her frustrations by throwing her knife at whatever stump or tree trunk was nearest the edge of the camp. She hit the farthest edge over and over until she sensed Kael behind her. He drew a blade from his belt and balanced it in his hand while she retrieved her own.

Briand was crackling with energy, all the emotions of the events of the last few days blended in her blood into a raging river of feelings. She felt borne on it, swept along.

"Need a few lessons, dragonsayer?" he asked.

Kael's blade hit the target, striking near the center. He was good.

She didn't say anything.

He stepped to the tree and reached for the handle, and then her blade was quivering in the space between his fingers. He paused, staring at it, and then he turned to look at her. Only the slightest flick of his eyebrows betrayed his thoughts.

"You have been keeping secrets," he said.

She felt a pang of coldness. Secrets. She had too many secrets. "I make a point of maintaining my image," she said crisply. "Sometimes, that image portrays me as all bluster and no talent. But I didn't survive this long on my own without learning how to throw a knife. I like to practice with the edge of the target. It's surprisingly hard to get the exact ridge along the edge in the same place every time."

He pulled her knife from the trunk and beckoned to her with his other hand, a slow curl of his fingers and palm. "Come. Show me your skills, dragonsayer."

She took the knife from him. He held onto it a moment, looking into her eyes, and she felt the heat of his attention and the challenge there to her toes. When he released the knife to retrieve his own, she moved away out of his reach.

Their fight was an argument without words. A conversation. A dance. He asserted, she rejoined. Back and forth. They circled, eyes locked on each other. He was as soft on his feet as a sand cat as he dodged her blows and returned with his own. A rare grin crossed his face as he swept her feet with his leg and knocked her down, and then he was over her, his blade at her throat, metal touching skin when she swallowed. His face hovered inches from her own, and then his smile faded, and his gaze passed over her face once before he drew back.

Briand sat up, heart pounding, lips tingling from the feel of his breath on them, her whole body one hungry pulse. She cleared her throat and sheathed her knife. Kael went to check the horses, and she gathered wood for the fire.

Nath had prepared a stew from whatever he could find in the saddlebags, and the resulting concoction tasted like shoes. Tibus rumbled good-naturedly that if Nath cooked as well as he talked, they'd eat like kings, and Maera claimed that the supper made her want to vomit. Then she did vomit into the bushes behind the horses, with the discreet efficiency of someone who had probably ingested poison on more than one occasion.

"Maera?" Nath asked, concerned.

"I'm fine," she said calmly as she returned to the fire, wiping her mouth and adjusting her hair.

Kael was silent, locked up in his thoughts even as he kept his attention on both the fireside conversation and the surrounding countryside. When the congenial bickering had settled down to grunts as they watched the fire burn to coals, he rose.

"I'll take the first watch," he said.

Briand found her gaze returning to his shape on the hillside, outlined by night sky. Nath stirred the coals, sending sparks into the sky, and Kael's profile was briefly illuminated in the light thrown from the fire. He had taken the letter from his father out and had it in his hand, but he wasn't looking at it. He was looking at the stars, his head tipped back.

Something clenched in her at the sight of that letter.

The others drifted toward sleep, but she couldn't. She rose from beside the fire and headed for the edge of the camp, pulled by an inexplicable impulse to pick at his thoughts. He was always so guarded and silent. She wanted to provoke him to words. She wanted to see him angry, because at least it would be something. She'd seen passion on his face at the inn, and it had been intoxicating.

The heat of the flames on her cheeks was cooled by a stiff wind, and she exhaled. The air tasted clean here, like sage and old stone.

Kael put the letter away before she reached him.

"Back to spar again?" The sound of his voice sent a shiver over her skin.

She sank down beside him. "You ought to throw that letter away."

He lifted an eyebrow without turning his head. He had a tiny scar as thin as a hair that traced along the edge of his hairline. She wanted to touch it.

"It motivates me," he said.

"There are better motivations, surely."

"What do you suggest instead, Catfoot?"

She was surprised that he was even listening to her. She took a moment to consider her answer.

"Honor," she said.

He laughed. "*You* talk to me of honor?" But he did not say it unkindly. Just honestly.

She shrugged. "It seems to matter to you. What matters to me? Loyalty. Love."

She felt a flush at the last word. She could feel him studying her.

"I know you love the prince," she said.

He was silent.

She held out a hand. "I think you should let me carry it instead. I won't... I won't read it. But you shouldn't keep it. You should carry other words. Better words."

He gazed at her hand, outstretched between them. She wanted to withdraw it in the silence that followed, but she persisted.

Kael shook his head. "Thank you, dragonsayer, but no."

His sudden pulling away confused her. Feelings crowded inside her, thick and heavy, and she returned to her bedroll without another word, feeling foolish for even trying.

~

"His feelings are not as impenetrable as he pretends them to be," Maera said in her ear the next day as Briand found herself scrutinizing Kael over the back of her horse as she saddled it. He gave her the feeling of dark water, with possibility of deadly things beneath.

Briand looked over her shoulder at the other woman, pricked by her words. Were hers?

"What do you mean?" she said, feigning ignorance, but in a halfhearted way. Briand liked Maera, because Maera didn't try to get Briand to trust her, and that seemed honest somehow, the admission that Maera

233

made no illusions to being anything but a devious sort of person.

"He likes you," Maera said. "It frightens him."

Briand didn't know what to say about that.

Maera smiled. "Oh, he's a nightmare to try to untangle, but once you start to understand his childhood and what he's been through, it all becomes astonishingly far easier to understand than I am. Many, many men and women have tried and failed to understand me." She winked.

"Nath would say you are merely Tasnians."

"Nath," Maera stated with an eye roll, "is prejudiced against those from the west."

Despite her cheerful demeanor, Maera was green about the lips, and when she mounted her horse, she paused a moment to steady herself. She pressed one hand to her side and shut her eyes.

"Are you well?" Briand asked.

"Just an old injury flaring up," Maera said, opening her eyes again with a sigh. "The climate here bothers it."

~

The land grew drier, lanced by the occasional eddy on its way the sea, the water a shocking green in the midst of the cracked soil. Stones pushed up from the earth like spikes driven through flesh. The vegetation clawed at them, all thistles and sharp jagged points and cacti.

At last they reached the city of Jaseel, carved from the stones of the canyons. The houses and markets were yellow with dust, the roofs jutting from the walls of the rock canyon at sharp angles, the windows like the eyeholes of a skull. After the wide skies and windblown plains of Estria, Sythra seemed crowded and hard. Even the faces of the people in the streets were lined and cracked by the relentless sun. Everyone seemed plagued by either lethargy or resignation.

"This city was once filled with Tyyrian traders, before their entrance to Austrisia became prohibited," Nath said in her ear. "They crossed the land bridge into Sioban south of here. Their trade brought most of the income before, so the city has withered in their absence."

Kael led them to an inn and rented a room for them to wait in while he disappeared with Nath to trade the horses for a carriage. Briand spent the hours pacing, while Tibus bickered with the innkeeper over the price of mead and Maera curled herself in the middle of the large bed.

When Kael and Nath returned, carrying bags of garments, Maera was sweating and shivering.

Briand turned to greet them. "Maera is sick."

"I'm fine," Maera gritted out. Then she cried out in pain, her body scrunching into a fetal position beneath the covers.

Kael laid down the garments and crossed to the bed. He crouched beside her and pressed a hand on her forehead. He pulled back the blanket and gently removed her hands from her stomach. "Does it hurt here?"

She inhaled sharply. "Yes."

"Get a doctor," Kael said over his shoulder. "Quickly."

THIRTY-TWO

BRIAND WATCHED MAERA writhe in pain while Tibus left without a word to fetch a doctor as Kael had ordered.

To Briand and Nath, Kael said, "Get the innkeeper to boil water. We'll need clean cloths as well. Hurry."

Maera turned her head toward the edge of the bed, and Kael grabbed the bowl there and helped her lean over to vomit in it. She was the color of a corpse, her hair wet with sweat against her scalp. She made a sobbing sound as she heaved.

"Go!" Kael said without looking up.

Tibus returned with a doctor while Briand was carrying up the cloths. Tibus took the cloths from her and followed the doctor into the room. Nath and Briand waited in the hall, listening to Maera moan faintly through the wall.

Tibus left and returned once, carrying a vial of something. He exchanged a few words with Nath that Briand couldn't hear.

A moment later, Maera screamed. Briand bolted up, and Nath sighed.

"Sit down, dragonsayer. There's nothing we can do. The doctor is there with her. Kael has seen this thing before."

She licked her lips. "Is it... a baby?"

Nath stared at her in surprise for a beat before barking a laugh. "Lords, no. Have you ever seen a woman in labor before, dragonsayer?"

She hadn't. She flushed, nervous and irritable. "I know there's a great deal of pain—"

"Yes, and a very large stomach, and lots of other symptoms for months beforehand."

"My mother didn't know she was carrying me until she had the pains of labor," Briand retorted. "She was thin as a reed. Not everyone has a large stomach before giving birth."

"Well, he would have sent for a midwife if she was about to deliver a child. Don't be a dolt."

"Just tell me what's wrong with her," Briand said.

"She has an inflamed organ," Nath said. "A rather useless one she can live without. They treat it often in Tasna, although it's not well-known outside the capital. A very new treatment. But Kael's seen it before. His brother experienced a similar affliction."

"What are they going to do?"

"They'll cut it out," Nath said matter-of-factly, as if saying the doctor was going to trim Maera's fingernails.

A wave of nausea swept over Briand. "Will she...?"

"Live? That remains to be seen." He pressed his lips together, and she saw then that he was terrified despite his glib words.

Another hour passed, and then the doctor emerged with blood on his shirtsleeves and sweat on his upper lip, carrying a bloodied bag. He was followed by Tibus and Kael. The doctor departed, and Nath and Briand rose. Tibus accompanied the doctor downstairs, and Nath slipped into the room while Briand hovered at the door, her stomach flopping as she met Kael's exhausted eyes.

"How is she?" Briand asked.

"Sleeping," Kael answered. "The physician sedated her."

"And he... successfully treated her?"

"He did." Kael rubbed a hand over his eyes. "She needs rest. She's in no condition to move."

Footsteps rang out behind them.

"Sir," a voice said, and one of the barmaids dropped a curtsey. She held out a letter. "This just came for you."

Kael opened the letter and scanned the contents. His mouth thinned.

"Get Tibus and Nath. We need to speak at once."

~

They discussed the plan while Maera slept in the bed, her hair inky against the pillow and her cheeks pale as bleached bone.

"I've received word from the prince," Kael said. "We must move immediately. Kul's gala is tomorrow, and Prince Jehn meets with the Serpent Queen in mere days. There is no time to wait for another event. We shall proceed as planned."

"But Maera—" Nath began.

"The dragonsayer will have to play the part instead."

She didn't know what to say. She'd promised him she'd stay. She'd see this through. But he was mad if he thought she could do this.

But what other choice did they have?

The dress fit her. She wasn't as curvaceous as Maera, but the fabric seemed to find appropriate places to cling to anyway. The layers of lace swung around her feet, lending her an air of grace.

Tibus grunted. "You look good, dragonsayer."

Nath tipped his head to one side and nodded.

"Don't be so shocked," Briand said with a laugh. But she was shocked at her reflection too. She turned back and forth, bemused at the image of herself that reflected back.

Kael cut his eyes away when she looked at him. "It will be sufficient. We'll need to hire a maid for your hair and other grooming tomorrow."

Tomorrow.

Her gut curled into a hard ball.

THIRTY-THREE

ARON KUL WAS not a man who liked to wait. In fact, he might call impatience his greatest flaw. It was the thing that most plagued him after his nervous fits. No, that was a lie. He lied to himself quite a bit, didn't he? Perhaps *that* was his greatest flaw.

The guards watched him as he read his letters over tea, sorting through correspondence from suitors and the latest news from the capital. His guards were always watching him that way, as if he were about to turn into a snake before their very eyes. He knew they whispered about him, that they called him the Butcher. That all the nation called him the Butcher.

His hand shook as he poured one of his powders into his glass and mixed it with water. Everything was prepared, now simply waiting for the gala to begin was straining his nerves. He swallowed the concoction and then gulped tea to wash away the bitterness on his tongue. Soon, the powder would work its effects and he would lose a little of the edge to his thoughts. Just enough to make him palatable to his guests, just enough to keep him from shying at shadows and jumping whenever the servants entered the room.

"Lord Kul," his steward said from the door, bowing. "The guests will arrive soon. Should I help you get dressed?"

Ever since his breakdown last year in Tasglorn, they'd all been treating him like a child. Giving him powders to keep him calm, suggesting he marry to distract him, sequestering him at this estate. Sending officials to check on him like a nursemaid looking in on her charge in his nursery.

He tried to make a scoffing noise and giggled instead. The powder was taking effect. He felt drowsy. He stood, knocking over his tea, and the guard reached out to assist him. Kul stepped away from the outstretched hand, stung by a flash of memory of a hand similarly outstretched, the fingers curled and the nails glinting as he stared in horror. "No," he said. "I'd rather... I'd rather not."

The guard lowered his arm. The steward came and steered him into the hall.

Kul stopped short. There, standing by the staircase, were three robed figures. Seekers. He pressed a hand to the wall to steady himself.

"I didn't realize you'd be coming so soon," he said. "I thought it wasn't going to be another several weeks."

They turned. The tallest one he recognized. Auberon, that young, ambitious Seeker who had been making gossip in the capital among Cahan's appointed.

Auberon swept a bow, which might have carried a hint of sarcasm, but Kul couldn't be sure with the powder in his bloodstream now. "Greetings, Butcher," he said. "I had reason to come early. I knew you wouldn't mind."

Of course he minded. And he hated that nickname. Kul smiled anyway.

"Your home is very festively decorated," Auberon observed. "Did you anticipate our arrival?"

"Gala," Kul said. The words tumbled out of him, nervous and giddy. "I'm hosting a gala."

"Ah, yes. Your quest for marriage. I recall." Auberon flexed his mouth in a smile. "You have time to accommodate us beforehand, I presume?"

That smile was wolfish. Kul nodded.

"Prince Cahan sends his love," Auberon said, and stripped off a glove. He looked at the steward, who was grim and silent beside Kul. "Is there a private place to do this?"

A shudder seized Kul, but he followed obediently. He knew what happened when he was not obedient.

~

Afterward, Kul sat reeling in his chair. He was always dizzy after the examinations, and the powder wasn't helping. Auberon was frowning over him.

"Didn't like what you saw?" Kul said, trying to sneer and slurring instead.

"Well, it was very indistinct," Auberon replied. "Your medicines make it so tiresome to read you. Your thoughts become glued together like wet paper. I'll have to try again later to find what I want."

"What are you looking for?" Kul murmured. "Perhaps I can help you find it."

"Ah," Auberon said. "You know better than to ask that." He looked around the room. They were in one of Kul's many ballrooms, this one with a length of glass windows that overlooked his Poisoned Gardens. "Now, where can I find your wine cellar?"

~

By the time the sun began to set, the party was in full swing, lights glowing and the music making Kul's head hurt. The powder had worn off enough that he felt cognizant of the world around him, and reality intruded too sharp and loud. He circled the room, making small talk with guests whose faces and names he didn't bother to learn. They were leeches, all of them, here for the food, the gossip. Jaseel was full of sleepy, exiled has-beens, lulled into a dreamlike state by the heat and the sea. They made him long for Tasglorn, full of ambitious, restless, brilliant men and women studying at the universities or rising through the ranks of Cahan's army. Always someone to discover, something to study.

Kul didn't want to think about what that made him, since he was a citizen of Jaseel too now. And thinking about Tasglorn made him want more powder to dull his senses.

He circled the room again, pausing by the tables laden with food to make sure they were arranged correctly. He didn't take anything to eat for himself—he never ate at parties. Too easy to be poisoned, and besides, he didn't like an audience when he was chewing and swallowing. It had been one of his quirks in Tasglorn—the man who never ate at the dinner parties he hosted. Here, no one seemed to even notice.

That was when he saw her.

She was slight, almost waifish, with a lean face and dark, curling hair drawn up in an elaborate style of buns and swirls. Her dress was green and made him think of the women of Tasglorn, with their long sleeves, sweeping trains, and cunning folds of fabric at the neck and wrists. He'd always had a bit of an interest in capital fashion, finding it beautiful. Unfortunately, every woman in Sythra seemed to wear the same curtain-like loose dresses.

She carried a fan—she was probably unaccustomed to the heat, he imagined—and when she saw him, she paused and hid half her face behind the fan as if shy. He found this intriguing, although he had no doubt she was anything but shy. Tasglornians rarely were, and he guessed from her clothing that she was from Tasglorn.

She curtsied when he approached, still keeping her face obscured by her fan. Her eyes were guarded, opaque, and he was dazzled by the spark of defiance he saw in their depths.

"My lady," he said, bowing. "May I ask your name?"

She extended one slender hand and placed her fingers in his. "Lady Cait Barria," she said. Her voice was husky, almost gruff, and it sent a thrill through him. "Did you receive my letter?"

Ah, she was one of the candidates seeking marriage. His heart beat a little faster. He kissed her fingers while he searched his mind for any recollection of a Cait. The blasted powders interfered with his memory sometimes.

"Of course," he lied. "But refresh my understanding, my dear."

"I've just arrived in Jaseel from Estria."

"Estria," he repeated, surprised. "I would have sworn you hailed from Tasglorn. You have an air of the capital to you."

She smiled, a thin kind of smile accompanied by an arch of her eyebrow that made him wonder what she could be thinking. Lords, this creature was fascinating to him. She was such a contradiction. "I have been told such things before. Perhaps I'm just an old soul."

"So you've never been to Tasglorn?"

She paused. "I have not. Does that disappoint you?"

"Well," he said, assessing his feelings. "It makes me long to see you in such a setting."

Two men lingered near her, both dressed in nondescript gray clothing, plain enough that he didn't think they were noblemen.

"Your guards?"

"Forgive me, but I feel more secure with them near me. You understand."

He did understand. This was a woman after his own heart. "And how do you find Jaseel?"

She glanced about. The place between her eyebrows wrinkled. "Hot. Dusty. Very dry."

He laughed. She said it as though someone had sucked the moisture from the air just to vex her.

"And your home?" he asked. "Do you miss it?"

Her face froze for a moment, and his imagination spun at that little flick of expression before she smiled again. Was she banished for some misdeed? He was hungry to know.

"I miss elements of my old life," she said. "But I can never truly go home again, not anymore."

He grasped her hand and bowed over it. "My lady," he said, "I understand completely."

Was that relief in her eyes? "This party is making me feel crowded. Do you want to talk somewhere quieter?"

He swept his hand to indicate the room. "Name a place, and we will go there."

She smiled coolly, her face still half-hidden by her fan. "I'm so very interested in your Poisonous Gardens. Show me?"

Better and better. Most women he'd seen so far feared his contraptions. They didn't understand why such things were necessary for him to have, why his safety—and sanity—demanded it. But he could tell at once that this woman would understand. She was scanning the room with the air of one accustomed to taking note of the exits, and she had a nervous quality to her, like a wild animal that had been cornered and was deciding whether to hide or strike back. He found it exhilarating.

"Come," he murmured, drawing her toward the doors. "Tell me, do you realize how lovely you are?"

She chuckled, or coughed. He wasn't sure.

Outside, the evening air was heavy with heat and kissed with the scent of moisture from his deadly water gardens. He stopped at the balustrade and turned to the young woman, who finally lowered her fan enough that he could see her entire face. She was pretty, but not too pretty. He liked it. He extended his hand to indicate the bloodtrees in the garden below, their leaves glimmering in the light of sunset as they shivered in the breeze like flames. "My collection of bloodtrees."

Of course, only some of them were bloodtrees. Most were look-alikes, there to frighten potential assassins away. But she didn't have to know that.

She studied the trees gravely. The place between her eyebrows pinched. He couldn't tell if she was impressed or disappointed.

He was fascinated with her.

She moved closer to the rail and rested her arms on it. Her shoulders were thin, her neck slender as a bird's. He had cut open a young woman with her physique once before, a lovely girl with the most beautiful spleen.

He wondered what this woman's spleen was like.

She seemed to have forgotten him, so he placed a hand on her wrist. "What do you think of my collection?"

She flinched at his touch. Kul frowned.

"Magnificent," she said, but it sounded strained. Did she think his collection ghoulish? Or merely unimpressive? "They are very dangerous trees, aren't they?"

"A brush of their leaves can make a man's skin bubble," he said proudly. "It's truly a thing to behold."

She nodded. Definitely impressed, he decided. He saw the way her eyes cut to his guards by the door. "Do you think we could be more alone...?"

He waved a hand, and his guards retreated inside. Hers would be adequate, surely.

"Thank you," she said with a coy smile. "I hate to have strangers watching me. I'm used to my own guards, but..."

"I understand," he said. He did. Cahan's palace guard had always made his skin crawl. They were like a host of possessed statues, deadly and as quiet as a coming storm.

"Tell me more about your gardens," she said.

"I have dozens of other exotic trees and shrubs in the labyrinth," he said, waving a hand at the stone maze visible in the distance. "Vines that make the skin swell, flowers that emit a vapor to make you faint, thorns as long as your hand."

"Labyrinth?" She lifted her gaze to study the visible stone walls. "It sounds so romantic."

"Only if your idea of romance involves dismemberment and death." He paused, a little hopeful, but she didn't respond to that, so he continued. "It surrounds the house and forms much of the estate's grounds, to deter potential attackers." He threw in that last bit because she seemed like the type to be impressed by someone who attracted a little bloodlust. "Modeled after the one at Prince Cahan's castle. I helped him design his, you know."

One of her bodyguards, standing near the door, sneezed.

She raised her eyebrows and leaned on her hand, head tipped to the left, eyes unfocused as she listened. Her other hand, resting on the balustrade, flicked at a fly, but she didn't even look away from his eyes as she did so. He felt a sense of triumph at having recaptured her interest.

"I was the chief physician of His Majesty until last year. Then I went on medical leave..." Suddenly, he found he didn't want to continue this story. It displeased him, and he wanted to feel pleasure in this moment.

He turned to go back toward the door. "Shall we return to the party?"

She grabbed his arm and pulled him back around. "Wait," she said, breathless. "I..." She paused as if deliberating, then leaned in and kissed his check abruptly.

He smiled. This was going very well indeed. "Let's go inside. Would you care to dance?"

"I don't dance often," she said. "But do you know how to play Dubbok?"

THIRTY-FOUR

KAEL SLIPPED BETWEEN the false bloodtrees as Briand and Kul disappeared inside, their voices fading. Briand had signaled him from the balcony, where she had a high enough view of the bloodtrees and their uppermost leaves to determine which were real. How fortunate that he'd seen fit to train her in the difference in Yeglorn, just in case. He thrust through the thick reddish leaves that formed a curtain between the palace and the rest of the gardens. If Briand was wrong, he'd be lying on the ground in agony in a matter of seconds.

His hand trembled as he shoved a vine away, and he counted in his head. Twelve heartbeats. No pain overwhelmed him. He didn't stumble or fall. His skin didn't turn red with boils.

The dragonsayer had chosen correctly. He could have kissed her stubborn, snappish mouth with relief and pride.

A snarl of thorned trees with barbs as long as his fingers reached out to snag him. He ducked low, the thorns scraping his skin and catching on his shirt. Ahead, he could see the wall of the labyrinth. An arched doorway opened to a path mottled with shadow.

Kael didn't hesitate as he stepped into the heart of the poisonous gardens. There wasn't time for fear.

He slipped through the paths, following the route he'd memorized. He paused to break off the long, spiny branches of a sickly green shrub, careful to keep the tips away from his skin.

When he reached the center of the labyrinth, the sound of water met his ears. He paused to strip off his belt and cloak. In the water ahead, he could see the dark shapes of shivsharks slipping through the water amid the splash of fountains. Fins sliced the surface as they passed.

He gripped the spines like swords in both hands and dove into the water.

~

Briand's mind rioted with anxiety as she stepped back inside, arm in arm with Kul. Her diversion on the balcony had worked. Kul hadn't noticed Kael slipping between the trees toward the labyrinth. Now, she needed to distract him for a little while longer. Preferably in a way that didn't involve kissing.

There was just one problem.

Auberon.

She'd spotted the Seeker right as she'd made her approach toward Kul. She had no idea why he was here. He hadn't invaded her dreams for days. Had he been tracking them, or was fate that cruel?

It had been too late to do anything but continue the plan, although she'd been so stiff with shock at seeing her former captor she'd barely been able to remember her instructions from Kael. The Butcher seemed to think her fear was some form of demure seduction, and Auberon hadn't noticed her with the fan blocking her face. He was too busy drinking wine and looking bored with the proceedings.

So far, everything was working, but she was trembling beneath her silken skirts. She felt like a mouse in a rat catcher's shop.

She snapped her fan back open as they stepped inside, using it to hide her face again in case any of the Seekers were looking her direction. Nath and Tibus stepped after her at a demure distance, playing the part of bodyguards.

"Dubbok?" Kul was saying in her ear. She'd blurted out the idea after he'd suggested dancing. She hadn't studied any Tasnian dances well enough to pass for a lady. That was supposed to be Maera's realm, after all. But she could play Dubbok with the best of them. Perhaps holding the cards in her hands would impart her with an extra sense of confidence.

Thankfully, Kul seemed intrigued and amused by the suggestion. He steered her toward a smaller room and signaled to a servant. "The lady wants to play Dubbok. Bring me a deck."

A few of the other guests showed some curiosity as they settled at a table. Dubbok, after all, was mostly a game for soldiers and dockhands. Watching a lady in a satin dress shuffle the cards seemed to amuse and bewilder them. Whispers filled the air behind fans and hands. But she had Kul's undivided attention, and that was the goal.

She dealt the hand. "I presume you know how to play?"

"My dear," Kul said, "I am brilliant at this game. Cahan loves it, you know."

"Well," she said, arching a brow in a way she'd seen Maera do when the spy was feeling superior, "have you ever played the guttersnipe version?"

He grinned, intrigued. "My dear," he said. "I hear it's only played by cutthroats and rapscallions. How could a lady like you know such a version of the game?"

Step one: get them to underestimate you.

"I've watched my brother play it, and he's the most rapscallion of them all." she said. She spun the cards in her cupped hands, making them dance. "Besides, I like to try new things, and Jaseel seems the perfect place to play a game for ruffians."

He laughed. He seemed to like it when she insulted Jaseel. She made a note of it.

"Shall we see if I am as clever as I imagine myself to be?" she said.

He grinned. "I should warn you, my lady, I am very good with cards. I am good with anything involving my hands."

She mustered a flirtatious smile even though his boast brought to mind his title the Butcher. "Prove it."

The clock on the wall behind him ticked loudly. She took a deep breath to stem the wild beating of her heart and dealt the cards. She looked at her hand. Nothing exceptional.

Across the table, Kul wrinkled his brow and drummed his fingers on the table.

The Seekers were in the other room. Kael was carrying out his part of the plan. And the Butcher of Tasglorn sat across from her, smiling at her as if she were already his.

254

The game was a blur. She played recklessly, instinctively, watching Kul's face instead of the cards. She wasn't playing for money. She was playing for her life.

She studied her hand. A waif and a knight. Kul played a card. A sovereign. He beamed. He thought he'd won.

She bit her lip. Her waif could assassinate his sovereign by the rules of this version, something most people forgot.

But sometimes winning meant losing first.

She chose to play the knight, who was loyal, and lost the game.

A guard came hurrying in to whisper in Kul's ear as she laid down her final card.

Kul's triumphant smile faded at what the guard said. His eyes snapped to Briand's. He rose with a crisp glance around him at the other guests, who were applauding politely at his victory.

"My dear," he said to Briand, his expression blank. "I've just heard some terrible news."

She tried to swallow, but her throat was too dry. She laid down her cards facedown and rose.

"Perhaps we ought to take this conversation to a more private location," she said.

He studied her a long moment. "All right. Bring your guards," he said.

They swept out of the room and down a staircase where sound was muted except for the echoing of their footsteps. Briand kept her eyes on Kul as more of his men stepped from a hall and surrounded her, Tibus, and Nath, hemming them in.

At the bottom of the staircase, Kul stopped. Two guards stepped from a shadowy nook, supporting a bloodied Kael between them. Water ran from his clothing and hair. A bruise was forming around his left eye. His lip was split.

He looked straight at her, his gaze an arrow straight to her heart. She wanted to run to him, but she stayed where she was.

Kul barked an order, and the men forced Kael to his knees. He didn't fight them.

"I understand from the guards at the entrance to my manor that this man accompanied you," Kul said, turning to Briand. He looked hurt, angry. "He was found in my labyrinth, swimming in one of my water gardens. Care to offer an explanation for this outrage that might soften my reaction?"

Briand licked her lower lip. She felt like the waif, surrendering. "No."

"No?" He stepped closer, lowering his voice a little. "I thought we understood each other," he said, his expression promising mercy.

Step two: Make your opponent eager to defeat you.

She closed her eyes briefly. "I understand that you are a sick, sad man who lost favor with his master."

Kul drew back as if she'd slapped him, his face hardening. "Search them and then lock them up. I'll deal with this after the party." He rubbed a hand over his mouth. "I need my powders," he said aloud to no one in particular.

They were marched down a passage and shoved into a cell with stone walls. Water seeped down the side of one in a thick, dark stain.

The door slammed behind them, and they were alone.

THIRTY-FIVE

KAEL WIPED BLOOD from his chin. He stepped to the door and listened as the soldiers walked away.

"The Seekers are here," Briand hissed. "Three of them, including Auberon."

It had all been part of the plan to be caught. According to the lore, the entrance to the caves was beneath in the dungeon, and getting through the guards would have required them to fight their way in. This way, Kul delivered them right to where they needed to go. Kael had swum through the water gardens earlier and dropped the tools through the grate that emptied into the dungeon waste pipes.

Everything was going according to plan, except for one thing. One thing that could ruin everything and get them all killed.

The Seekers.

Nath was already in a panic about them. He pressed against the wall, his face pale and his hands shaking. Kael took him by the arms. "Look at me, Nath," he commanded. Nath raised his face obediently. He was trembling violently.

"You're going to be all right," Kael said firmly. "Stay with us. Nath. Breathe. Focus on me. Tibus, get those tools. We need to start breaking through this wall."

But before anyone could move, the door was flung open.

"Well, hello," Auberon said as he stepped inside, flanked by Kul's guards. "We meet again. I thought I'd lost you when you threw me from your mind," he said to Briand. "But fortunately, you escaped with your soldier friend here." He indicated Tibus with a flick of his fingers. "We had a bit of a struggle at the inn, and my Hunters were able to use his blood to track him here."

He said all this calmly as he lounged in the doorway, one shoulder leaning against the frame, his ankles crossed.

"What do you want from me?" she said, trying to distract him from the others. He thought he had them trapped. But if he tried reading Nath or Tibus, he'd learn their plans and all would be lost. They, unlike her and Kael, could not shield their minds from the Seeker's probing power. They could give everything away.

She had to keep him from reading them.

Auberon laughed. "Dear girl. I have great plans for you and your abilities. But you seem to have said something to anger Kul, so it might take some prodding on my part to get him to give you up. He holds the most magnificent grudges, you see."

"Please," she said, buying herself time with begging. She was willing to debase herself for Nath. "Please don't let them hurt us."

"The traitor will die," he said with a wave of his hand. "I can't help that, and I don't care to. The others likely will too, after I've seen their minds."

She had one card yet to play. She drew a quick, strangled breath.

"I have information," she said. "You might find it useful."

He peeled off one glove, ignoring her. "Hold the thin one down," he said to the guards, nodding at Nath.

Nath made a sound like an animal dying in a trap as the men dragged him forward. His eyes rolled back in his head.

"Wait," she cried out. "I am on a mission for the emperor of Bestane!"

Kael's head whipped around. Auberon's hand stopped an inch from Nath's face.

"A man came while I was in hiding," she continued. "He killed the Hermit who was keeping guard over me. He gave me a choice: death, or a promise of safety in exchange for... for going on this mission with the enemy and killing Kael."

For one aching moment, the room was silent. She could her heartbeat. Kael looked stricken. Nath whispered something under his breath.

"I'm confused," Auberon said pleasantly.

"I'll sum up for you: she's a guttersnipe willing to do anything to save her neck," Kael said without looking away from Briand.

Briand wanted to weep at the way he looked at her. As if she'd already sunk the knife into his chest.

"Ooh," Auberon said. "Intrigue. And self-preservation. I like that in a person. And I like this dramatic display. It's as good as one of the plays in the Theatre District. But why do you think I'd care about your lies to your friends?" Auberon drawled with a lift of his eyebrow. "Other than the delicious irony, of course?"

Briand's heart stumbled as she played her last card. The one meant for Auberon.

"Because the man who came was a Seeker."

"No lies," Auberon said. But the first hint of doubt showed on his face.

"It's not a lie."

Nath, Tibus, and Kael were still staring at her.

Overload the mind with shock and you can lock the Seekers out temporarily.

Had it been enough?

Auberon turned on Nath and slapped his bare palm against the tutor's forehead. Nath's eyes squeezed shut, and after a moment, Auberon hissed a curse and drew his hand back. "I shall return when your minds have cleared. Let me tell you what's going to happen when I do. I am going to figure out exactly what you know, all of you. Then I will turn your unfortunate friends over to Kul's guards. I hear they like to feed thieves to the sharks and take bets on who dies first. You and the traitor will come with me to Tasglorn. Our inquisitors have creative methods of making betrayers suffer. He will probably die trying to tear his own skin off."

He left the room in a swirl of cloak, followed by the guards. The door slammed shut, and Briand raised her gaze to the others.

They wouldn't look at her now.

"Kael," she said.

"Is it true?" His voice was raw.

"Most of it," she said.

His face closed up like a locked door. He turned away from her, and a pit opened up inside her. She grabbed his arm to stop him.

"Kael—"

He removed her hand. "Quickly," he said to the others. "We don't have much time before he returns."

"*Kael.* Listen to me."

He turned his burning gaze on her. She wanted to wither beneath it.

"I just saved this mission," she said. "You know what I did. If I hadn't, he would have discovered our plans to break out of here. He would have found the tools. At least this way, we have a little time."

"Time we shouldn't be wasting." He spoke in a monotone.

"This isn't like Drune," she hissed. "It isn't remotely the same."

"No?" He said it coldly.

She wanted him to argue with her. To fight her. Something other than this monosyllabic shut down.

"No," she said. "I didn't kill the Hermit. I thought the man was going to kill me, but instead, he offered me a deal. To kill you."

His eyes closed. "And the mission for Bestane? Our enemy?"

"That was a lie. There is no mission for Bestane, only the one with you. I thought it would create the most shock and cloud Nath's mind. To keep the true mission safe, Kael."

"But it's true that you accepted an order to kill me."

"I did it to survive! And I was never going to kill you. I never wanted any of you hurt. I left when I thought I was putting you in real danger, but you begged me to come back. You said you needed me. I was going to honor our deal and then leave forever."

Kael's eyes darkened at the memory. "Our deal," he repeated, as if the words were poisoning him by being in his mouth. He turned away. "We have a mission to finish, and no time for this conversation. Let's get to work."

She was broken in half by his dismissal, but she gathered herself back together. He was right. They had no time. Not now.

Tibus withdrew the metal rods from the grate, splashing water everywhere. Kael counted the stones until he found the right one, and then Tibus, Nath, and Kael set to work on scraping the mortar away. Kael worked until sweat poured down his face. He was utterly silent.

Briand stripped out of the cumbersome Tasnian gown. Beneath it, she wore trousers and the bodice Reela had made her. She left the shining pile of fabric on the floor by the door as she pulled the knives out of her hair, letting the locks tumble down around her shoulders. She slipped the knives into her belt and swiftly braided her hair away from her face.

The men drew back, and Kael kicked the stone. It slid into the wall, leaving a square hole in its wake. Kael reached into his shirt and withdrew the necklace engraved with the symbol, the one Drune described to her years ago, and it began to glow faintly as he whispered a word of magic over it. The light was enough to illuminate their steps as they squeezed through the entrance and into the passage beyond.

A gust of dank air fanned Briand's cheeks as she ducked into the passageway after Tibus. Her heart was in her throat. She was dizzy with anticipation as darkness enveloped them.

It was almost time now.

The stone lay broken on the ground at their feet. A ceiling of stone arched above them, hung with daggers of rock. Kael pointed forward, where a staircase wound down and down into the earth.

"This way."

They began to descend to the gloom. Sound echoed weirdly, every scuff of shoe or scrabble of pebbles reverberating and multiplying.

"Kael," Briand said, drawing beside him. "Please, listen to me."

"There is nothing more to say."

She wanted to shake him. She had to make him understand. "After you came for me in the inn—"

"I was an utter fool," Kael said harshly. "Forget anything I said or did that night. I thought you were more than a guttersnipe turned thief, but I was wrong."

She drew back, a flush covering her face. "You're right," she said, each word tasting bitter. "We've both been fools."

He didn't reply to that. "Nath," he barked. "Stay with the dragonsayer." And then he brushed past her, leaving her stinging.

She let him move ahead before she resumed walking again. Nath touched her arm. They didn't speak, but he stayed beside her as they continued to descend the staircase down, down, down into the dark.

Finally, Kael held up a hand to stop them. He pointed. Rising from the darkness was a door, set in the stone walls, round and ancient. Tibus and Kael struggled to drag it open. The stone grated along the floor in a scream of protest, stone against ancient stone. The darkness throbbed behind them, black and pulsating with the threat of attack, and the shadows seemed to watch them as they worked. She felt both blind and exposed.

Through the opening behind the round door, another set of steps descended down like the broken spine of a long-dead beast. Briand felt a fresh spasm of fear.

"These tunnels and catacombs were built by the ancients, just like the bridge," Nath whispered to her as they climbed through the hole. "Kael's necklace glows because we're in proximity to so much old magic. It's why the dragons linger here, they say. Can you feel them?"

She reached out in her mind. She was unsettled to her bones, but she didn't detect any thoughts that were not her own. Hers wheeled like birds in flight, her mind soaked with sorrow and burning with fury all at once.

"Not yet," she said.

The steps went down and down. It was too dark to see far, but judging from the echoes, they were in a great expanse of space now. Kael's light was a prick in the darkness. Once, something skittered away from them with a flurry of wings. Her stomach clenched, and she grabbed for her knife, but then the creature was gone. A soft groaning sound murmured around them, like the sound of settling rocks.

Suddenly, she could sense them. Their thoughts were flashes of fire in her mind, searing her as they blistered through her consciousness. Briand's feet stumbled on the steps. She grabbed Nath's arm.

"I feel them."

"Where?" He was alert now.

She gestured with one hand. "Below. I can't pinpoint it more than that, not right now."

She could feel their awareness of her. They were sensing her. They were wary of intruders. She gleaned flickers of memories—the snap of bone beneath her jaws, the taste of flesh on her tongue, hot blood and soft tissue. She was suddenly much bigger and hotter and rage flowed through her like heat at being disturbed. *She had to keep the offspring safe.* She was uncoiling herself, muscles unclenching after much sleep—

She wrenched herself free from the dragon's mind. She was falling. She leaned in to Nath, grateful for his presence, hurting from Kael's absence. The memories and sensations lingered like heat behind her eyelids. She tried to blink them away. The dragons' minds were still waiting below, like holes beneath her feet that she could not help but fall into. She shivered as a pain like lightning licked her mind.

"Dragonsayer?" Nath asked. "Are you all right?"

"They know we're here," she said for everyone to hear.

266

Kael looked over the side of the staircase into the nothingness beyond instead of at her as he spoke. His glowing necklace swung out over the dark. "Let's keep moving."

Her stomach curled into a fist, and then she was falling into the dragon again—

Heat. Her mouth was hot, and the air smelled of ash. She was moving now, crawling through the cavern, her vision strange and red. She felt the stone around her, the currents of air speaking to her, the heat and the cold of the land like another language on her scales.

They reached the bottom of the stairs. A floor spread away in a flood of stone, and they were ants on a frozen sea as they ran, the light of Kael's necklace bouncing and throwing light all around with every stride he took. Briand was in the darkness and then in a light so hot her clothing felt like flames against her skin and cold from the air fanning her face. She was scales and teeth and skin and hair. She could see the others ahead of her, and then she saw the redness again, and felt the hot, ancient rage of a thing awakened in the dark from a dreamless sleep.

The growl came creeping from the distance, a guttural groan that made them all pause. Her pulse drummed wildly in her throat. She pressed her fingers to her head.

"How... how much farther?" She was seeing bands of light.

"There," Nath said. "Ahead. See those buildings?"

More steps, these wide and shallow, led to a platform built into the wall. Stone structures. Ruins? The stone here glittered as if set with diamonds.

The company reached the steps, and then they were climbing on ahead. Briand's legs were numb, her hands shaking. She sank down on the steps and shut her eyes to better concentrate on the dragon filling her head with its consciousness.

It paused as if sensing her, and she *pushed* as she'd pushed against Auberon's intrusion into her mind. Trying to slow it. Trying to calm it.

Shhh, big lizard, she thought. You are not so angry. You are not so vengeful. We aren't here to hurt you or your children.

It raged in response, but she kept pushing, cajoling, insisting. Just like Sieya with a treat, she was firm.

The dragon paused again. It seemed perplexed with her interference. Concerned. She shook her head, and the dragon shook its head. She was bleeding into the dragon again, unsure where she ended and the fire beast began.

Then she was Briand again, with stone under her feet and human hands that she pressed against her face to rub at the throb of the dragon's consciousness scalding through her own in a thread of fire.

She heard the others scrabbling up the steps above to the top of the ruins. Grit rained down around her, prickling the skin of her arms. Her mind began to feel warm, as if a fire had sparked behind her eyes. She felt herself expanding again.

"Dragonsayer!" Nath called from far above. "Report?"

"Hurry," she ground out. The warmth was becoming uncomfortable. It spread to the edges of her skull. She reached up a hand and felt her hair, and she jerked her hand back at the blaze of heat seeping through her skin.

The dragon broke free of her mental restraint. Briand felt it like a snap in her mind. She cried out and reached for it again. Its confusion and anger at her interference washed over her.

She turned to look up at Kael and the others. They had vanished inside a broken doorway surrounded by a crumbling row of columns. The light from Kael's necklace flickered far away.

The edge of her sight turned red. A glow bathed the far reach of the cavern, the flicker of fire from dozens of mouths. She turned back to face the vast darkness of the cave, her heart leaping to her throat.

They were coming.

She was frozen, unable to stir or look away as the darkness rippled and crawled. The dragon that shared her mind was close, but the skittering sounds around her were closer.

The walls of the cave twitched. The throb of wings beat the air.

They were converging on the ruins. Like a swarm of mammoth bats they came, the size of horses, much smaller than the dragon at the bridge two years ago, but still deadly-looking, with curling tails and needle-like teeth and glowing, blinking eyes. Spines and stripes glowed faintly on some of them, while others were black as ink. One knocked her with its wings, and she tumbled over the side of the steps and into a crack in the stone, out of sight. She lay there a moment, breathing hard, listening to the rush of death approaching as fear choked her.

She wasn't strong enough. She didn't know how to do this. She was unskilled, untrained, and literally playing with fire. She could stay here, hidden and safe, and then make her escape. Crawl away while the dragons' attention was focused on the Monarchists. Make a new life. The Seekers would think she'd perished here with the others, if they found them.

Above, she heard the others. Their shouts rang out as they saw the horde surrounding them.

Hide, run? Or stay and fight?

"Dragonsayer?" Nath called. Then, in a panic, "Briand!"

She was not just a guttersnipe. She was not just Pieter's scrappy, unwanted niece, or the thrall of a thief-queen. She was Catfoot. She was the dragonsayer. And she would be a loyal friend to the last.

The strength to fight flowed from the realization. They needed her. She loved them. She realized she would never refuse their call for help, even if it cost her everything.

Briand drew one long breath and swung herself from the crack into the open. The dragons were all around her, the air reverberating with the sound of their scales against the stone and their wings against the air, their thoughts crowding into her mind like a shower of fiery sparks. She pressed both hands over her eyes at the agony of so much mental weight brought to bear on her. Her thoughts were on fire, her vision a blur.

Dimly, she heard Nath shout in alarm, "There're scores of them!"

She gathered a breath and pushed with her mind. It was like striking a mountain. Fear pulled at her. She reached inside herself again—how could she turn back a horde?

"Please, please," she muttered. "Listen to me."

One of the dragons exhaled a plume of fire, illuminating the cave. Her stomach coiled at the sight of them scuttling and fluttering overhead. There were dozens of dragons, all converging on the ruins.

She couldn't control that many. She couldn't begin to know how.

"BRIAND!"

It was Kael shouting this time. She looked and saw them pinned by the rocks. She ran for the steps. If she couldn't stop the dragons from here, at least she could put herself between them and her friends.

Briand began to climb.

Her mind was burning, her hands and legs shaking. She tried again to gather enough energy to harness the dragons, but she was hemmed in by their minds all around her. She kept climbing. She was Catfoot, after all. She'd escaped Seekers and survived flooded rivers. She had been kicked in the teeth by life enough to have learned how to keep going.

Her legs shook, and she stumbled onto her hands and knees. The rock steps tore into her hands, and she felt the blood seep down onto the stone as she dragged herself upward.

Another wave of flame lit the darkness above. She felt its blistering heat as she pulled herself to the top of the steps and pressed both hands against the glittering rocks. She looked up and caught a glimpse of Kael's face, desperate in the firelight, his eyes windows straight to his heart. He was not looking at the dragons. He was looking at her.

She had to save him.

On her hands and knees on the glittering rock, she pulled in, just as she'd done with Auberon that first time he'd tried to read her mind, and she choked on the power that surged through her. She gave one last push with her mind, and this time, the power shot of her like a shockwave.

The dragons reeled back as if knocked by a giant hand. They swirled overhead in masse, clicking and snarling. She kept pushing. Spots danced in front of her eyes, and sweat slicked her face and arms. The dragons poured upward into a tunnel, lighting it with fire as they went.

Then Nath was at her side, pulling her up, and Tibus had her other arm, and they were running down the steps. Tibus had a bag in his hands, and it thumped against her ribs.

"The treasure?" she gasped out.

He nodded.

"There's another one," she said between breaths. "A bigger dragon. I can still feel it."

Now that the others had fled, the quiet dread of the monster lay thick alongside her thoughts.

"We're getting out of here," Nath assured her.

Her legs were weak. She tripped against Nath and fell along with him, her chin smacking the stone, knees scraping. Then Kael was there, scooping her into his arms. He tucked her head beneath his chin, and her ear was against his heartbeat. It was wild against her cheek. She closed her eyes as he ran with her, saying nothing, his arms tense even as they cradled her. Tears seeped from beneath her eyelids as she tasted smoke in her mouth and the dragon drew her mind back like taffy pulled between two hands. It was searching for her. She let herself fall into the dragon's mind as Kael carried her.

She was dizzy from the ascent. Higher, higher. They reached the top, and her head was throbbing with the dragon's presence. She felt its fury as it moved in the caverns below. She panted with the strain of holding it back.

"Almost there," Kael said, his voice a rumble against her ear.

Then he stopped.

Briand opened her eyes.

Auberon stood in the corridor, blocking the way forward with his men.

THIRTY-SIX

AUBERON FACED THEM—the runaway traitor and his two unfortunate compatriots, and the mysterious girl with the impenetrable mind curled in the traitor's arms—with a smile.

"So clever. So resourceful, getting caught on purpose, hiding the tools for your escape in the pipes."

Judging by the dismay on their faces, this bit wasn't part of the plan.

"I see you and your friends have resolved your disagreements," he said to the girl. "Always a good thing to do before you die, I'm told."

She held his gaze without flinching. She was so fierce. He felt a flicker of fondness for that indomitable spirit, and regret that it would undoubtedly be broken soon. It must be broken. Not by him. He would do what he could to shield her until his questions were answered, but the Citadel would want her dead.

Kael stood stiff-backed, his eyes blazing with a light they hadn't shown during the months that he'd played lapdog to Calys and made fools of them all. He would pay for his crimes. Auberon's mouth curled. "If I was a merciful man, I would kill you now."

Kael stared back without speaking, defiant and drenched in sweat and grime. His men stepped closer to him as if their pitiful efforts would do anything to protect him. Auberon flicked his fingers, signaling to the men. They stepped forward.

"Don't," the girl said. Her voice was just a raw scrape of sound. "Don't come any closer."

"Or what?" Auberon said, grinning. "You'll bludgeon me with those stolen jewels? You've lost, girl. Accept it."

"I hope you've resolved all your disagreements," the girl said, and then she closed her eyes.

And the air behind her exploded with fire.

~

Briand let the dragon go, and it shot up toward them in a blaze of wings and fury, jaws open, flames licking from its tongue. She shoved back before it could reach them, and the dragon hesitated. She felt the heat of it blast around her and knew it was seething fire.

She blinked and saw that everyone else had fallen, from fear or the heat. Auberon was on his knees, staring at her in amazed terror.

"Dragonsayer," he breathed. "It's true."

She felt cold all over. Light danced at the edges of her vision. She was burning, but she couldn't feel it.

The dragon landed behind her with a shudder of the rock and a cloud of dust. It snarled, and Briand's ears popped. Sound was muffled. She could feel her heart pounding, her breath leaving her lungs, the dragon drawing in air to belch out flame. She shoved with everything she had to control the beast and pull it back.

Even if it killed her, she would finish this. She would save them. It was the least she could do to rectify how she'd drawn the Seekers here.

"Briand," she heard Kael shout.

She locked eyes with Auberon. She mouthed goodbye.

He scrambled up and back toward the tunnel without tearing his gaze from her and the dragon. Around him, his men were scattering.

She shut her eyes again. This time, she yanked at the dragon's mind instead of shoving.

The dragon unleashed its fire toward the Seeker and his men. The tunnel collapsed.

Everything went black.

~

Briand was washed in pain when she woke. Nath bent over her, murmuring her name. He shouted for Kael as she focused on him through the blur.

"The dragon?" she asked, trying to sit up. Her skin cracked as she moved. She felt scraped raw inside and out.

"Gone," he said. "What did you do?"

"I don't know."

Her hands were black with soot. Ash drifted in the air. The world was lit with soft orange from the embers around them, and the tunnel they'd come through had collapsed.

Then Kael was beside her, clasping her hand in his. One side of his jaw was blistered, the stubble of his chin singed, and sweat and ash streaked his face.

"Can you move?" he asked. The place between his eyebrows creased with worry as he looked down at her.

She shifted her legs experimentally. "I can."

"Are you in pain?"

She was. "It isn't so bad." She paused. "Does it look terrible?"

Kael shook his head. His eyes were soft. "Not so terrible."

Nath snorted. "Liar," he said softly. "You look like a cinder, dragonsayer. Whatever possessed you to take such a risk?"

She sighed. "I have many debts to repay." She met Kael's eyes as she said it.

"Hush," Tibus chided from where he sat on a rock, his elbows braced on his knees. He lifted his head to smile at her. "You saved our lives. Again."

Kael helped her up to a sitting position. His hands were gentle on her shoulders. "You're burned," he said. "How are you not roasted alive?"

"Dragonsayer magic?" she suggested with a rasp of a laugh that turned into a cough.

He shook his head in wonder. "Maybe."

"Kael," she whispered. "The Hermit—"

A shadow passed over his face. "You've proven yourself our friend and saved our lives, as well as the prince's chances for an alliance with Nyr, Briand. I will honor our agreement. I won't cause any harm to come to you."

"But there's more than what you know. Listen to me. The one who killed him... He dressed as a Seeker,

277

but the Hermit knew him as a Monarchist. He trusted him."

Kael's face hardened into stone. "Who was it?"

"I never saw his face, but he had a tattoo of a lion on his wrist. The Hermit called him Marl." She'd kept that information from Auberon. That, at least, she could offer him. She licked her lower lip, and it stung.

"I don't know the name."

Part of his left eyebrow had burned. She reached out to touch it, and he closed his eyes for a moment. His skin was hot beneath her fingertips.

Nath and Tibus pretended to be interested in the fallen rocks of the cavern beyond.

She traced his face down to his mouth, and he let her before he reached up and captured her hand carefully with his.

"We can't."

She froze at the expression on his face. Regret, or disgust? "What do you mean?"

"I might have engaged in some... lapses of judgment on this mission," he said. "But it cannot continue."

She flushed hot as she pulled her hand away. He might as well have slapped her. "I see."

"Briand..."

She shook her head, unable to speak for a moment. Every one of her limbs was stiff, and her jaw felt like stone.

Kael didn't speak either. They sat in silence.

Briand looked at the tunnel behind him, or where it had been. Blackened stones covered the entrance. They wouldn't be able to get through. "What now?"

"Use the dragons," he said. "They'll know if there's another way out."

She sighed. Her arms and legs hurt now, a burn like she'd been scraped all over her body. She was so tired, the hurt of his rejection turning to numbness that mingled with her exhaustion. The prospect of reaching for the dragons again made her want to vomit.

She closed her eyes. "If we escape, where will you go?"

"The court of the true prince," Kael said. He helped her to her feet, expressionless and remote now. Focused.

"Do you think Auberon survived?" she asked.

"If he did, he knows what you are now," Nath said, stepping to her other side. "All the more reason to get moving."

"We'll deal with it in time. First, we need to get out of here and to the safety of the prince's court." Kael said. "Come with us, Briand."

She turned to him, startled. "Even after the Hermit's death? Even after my link with the Auberon?"

"You didn't kill the Hermit," Kael said. "You drove Auberon from your head. And you risked yourself again and again to keep the rest of us safe."

She gazed at him, uncertain. Exhausted. Wary.

"I'll never be a Monarchist, Kael. That's not what I want."

But she followed him anyway as they started down the climb toward the promise of the sea, and escape.

ACKNOWLEDGEMENTS

Scott, for being my life-long companion, tireless supporter, and first reader of every manuscript. I love you.

My family (my parents, siblings, and wonderful in-laws), for talking about my books to practically every person you meet in every doctor's office and classroom between here and North Carolina, for cheering me on, and for acting like I'm famous. I love you guys.

H. Danielle Crabtree, for being an editing ninja of awesome.

My readers, for their faithful support and infectious enthusiasm. It means so much to me that you all love these characters. I love you guys!

Made in the USA
Columbia, SC
05 January 2021